COOKING UP CHAOS

LITTLE DOG DINER, BOOK 4

EMMIE LYN

Editor: Helen Page
Proofreader: Alice Shepherd
Cover Designer: Lou Harper, Cover Affairs

Sweet Promise press
PO Box 72
Brighton, MI 48116

For all my rescue dogs and cats who are the best friends ever.

ABOUT THIS BOOK

*A*utumn on the Maine coast is stunning, which brings the tourists out in droves. My restaurant, the Little Dog Diner, is teeming with them, thanks to the locally famous fall festival.

Usually that's a great thing... this year, however, the discovery of a dead body puts a damper on business awfully fast.

Add to that, the fact that the victim had a vendetta against almost every small business owner in town, and now I've landed right in the middle of the very long and tedious suspect list.

Looks like it's time to toss my apron aside and don the detective hat once more. Thankfully, Pip is more than ready to assist in this one, because if I didn't get to the bottom of this chaos quickly, it could be me getting cooked!

*T*rouble sat outside my bedroom door bright and early Thursday morning.

Literally — Trouble — with four paws, a loud yowl, and a one-eyed glare. At least, I assumed he was glaring. His paw swiped underneath the door, aiming for Pip's nose, so what other expression could have been on that creature's face?

Pip dodged the claws with grace, but her terrier focus must have lapsed for a second because I heard a yip over Trouble's yowl, and a spot of red bloomed on Pip's nose when she leaped back.

"I know you want to be friends, Pip, but Trouble hasn't adjusted to living with a Jack Russell terrier yet."

Trouble had patrolled the Misty Harbor Police

Station for at least a year. But when a new hire complained that the cat triggered her allergies, Trouble needed a new home and just my luck when my grandma Rose obliged.

Maybe I'd feel better if Trouble had a different name. I had enough strife on my own plate. This weekend promised to serve up an extra helping of stress with the Better Business Award getting everyone's attention, and Wilhelmina Joy, Misty Harbor's dedicated environmentalist, attacking us for littering the beach with single use packaging. Did I need any more trouble... the four-legged or two-legged variety?

I looked at Pip. Her only trouble at the moment involved her breakfast. She wouldn't get any until I got myself in gear. So, I slipped into my running shorts, t-shirt and shoes and followed her downstairs to the kitchen.

I was suspicious of the complaint about Trouble. Josie Hiller, the new dispatcher at the police station, claimed to be allergic, but word on the street was that she just didn't like cats. When Rose heard of the dilemma, it only took her a second to rescue Trouble and bring him back to Sea Breeze, the home I shared with her and Pip.

Yup, I, Dani Mackenzie, had a new four-legged

houseguest, and I was afraid this guy was exactly what his name implied—trouble—in the form of disrupting the current balance at home.

Like I said, Pip wanted to be friends with the ornery tabby cat even if Trouble gave no indication of reciprocating. But, if Pip was anything, she was determined, so I opened my door and let the fun begin.

Did I say fun? Well, it's all in the perspective, I guess. Mine.

With the door open, Trouble's bravado disappeared in a gray blur down the stairs with a slightly bigger white blur, named Pip, close behind.

I wasn't worried.

Pip knew that Trouble was part of our family now and she wouldn't dare hurt a hair on the cat's cantankerous head.

None the less, Trouble took refuge on Rose's lap, with his green, one-eyed glare daring Pip to come close enough for a swipe on her nose.

Pip knew the game and kept her distance, a safe paw swipe away, and then some.

I, on the other hand, tried to make peace. I gave Trouble a pat, but he rewarded my effort with a hiss. Maybe he knew I played favorites, in any case, I scooped up Pip, left Trouble to Rose's cooing and stroking, and made my way into the kitchen.

"Things aren't the same anymore, are they, Pipsqueak?" I said as I prepared her breakfast of ground chicken and rice. She stared at me over her food bowl, her head tilted to one side, her ears angled forward, and her bright eyes holding the expectation of an adventure or… food.

"Want to join me for our run on the beach before I head to the Little Dog Diner?" I asked Pip. She'd have to stay here with Rose and Trouble so a romp on the beach was the least I could do. I'd have just as much fun, of course, even if I didn't spend my time harassing the seagulls or thinking I could catch a wave, Pip's daily obsession.

She took her time with her breakfast while I pulled on a fleece layer over my shirt to ward against the crisp, cool October morning.

"Ready?" I asked Pip when I returned downstairs.

She ran to the door.

"I'll have tea and scrambled eggs ready when you get back, Dani," Rose said without taking her hand off Trouble. He had his one eye slit and a purr of happiness rumbling from his chest. I think he thought he'd died and gone to heaven after whatever his earlier years had thrown at him.

No one knew his history or what happened to his missing eye. I just knew that going forward, without one ounce of doubt, that Trouble had settled in at Sea Breeze. For Good.

Pip would have to adjust.

A few stretches on the patio later, and I followed Pip down the steps to the beach that bordered Blueberry Bay on the coast of Maine.

Like many mornings, fog had settled over the water, but I could run along the beach with my eyes closed if necessary. Pip, too. She had dashed so far ahead of me I could barely see her neon yellow bandana flapping in the distance. I needed to pick up my pace if I wanted to catch her, but I didn't. I needed this early morning run time to think.

Not always a good thing.

Lily, my best friend since forever, and no longer a partner with Rose and me at the Little Dog Diner, recently started her own catering business. Hence, I had to train two people to take her place. Chad and Christine Golden came highly recommended by my grandmother, and I liked both of them a lot, but they weren't Lily. She and I had our own brand of silent communication. We could work side by side and never get in each other's way. Training two new people was proving to be a lesson in exhaustion.

In addition, on Friday night, Misty Harbor would announce the Best Business Award. Rumor had it that, of the four finalists, the Little Dog Diner had the lead. The whole weekend would showcase the best of Blueberry Bay—a blessing and a curse rolled into one giant high energy stressathon—with all of the local high mucky mucks making appearances.

On the plus side, the event meant lots of free advertising for the diner. On the downside, some of the other businesses in town had started to cry foul, each of them furious, I'd heard, because I was the front-runner for this plum honor. They all screamed unfair advantage since Rose, being my grandmother and all, was one of the sponsors of the weekend event.

Boo-hoo, I said to myself. If I won, it was because I deserved the honor, not because Rose swayed the organizers' decision. She was too honest to interfere. I planned to take home the thousand-dollar prize plus the gold Best Business Award, which I'd proudly display in the Little Dog Diner.

You'd think that was more than enough on my plate of goodies, but no, life had recently thrown

Wilhelmina Joy at me. A do-gooder on a mission to keep Blueberry Bay clean of single use items. Though why she had the name Joy attached to her, escaped me. Whoever gave her that name never saw this angry activist at work. I admired her goal, but her style left me cold. Unfortunately, she'd taken a break from protesting at the Savory Soup & Sandwich Café to protest right in front of the Little Dog Diner.

Jeez, Louise, I couldn't catch a break lately.

I decided I could no longer avoid a friendly chat with Wilhelmina Joy.

With that decision made, I kicked up my speed, hoping to leave my problems buried in the sand. I caught up with Pip at the rocky point below the Kitty Point Lighthouse where we always turned back toward Sea Breeze, my beacon above the early morning fog.

As much as I tried, I could never beat Pip back to the steps that led from the beach to my home. Huffing and laughing, I climbed up to the terrace behind her. I had exactly ten minutes to shower, change, and gobble down my breakfast before rushing to the diner.

Let the trouble begin.

2

I drove faster than I should have in my dark green MG. This early, I doubted I'd run into police who might nab me for speeding. That's if this was one of my rare lucky days... apparently, not today.

Detective AJ Crenshaw, born and bred in Misty Harbor, had gone through school with me. My bad timing had me zipping right past the intersection of his road and his route to the police station.

Like I said when I woke up... trouble found me today—either the four-legged variety with a capitol T or the bad-luck type with flashing blue lights.

I pulled over, and AJ walked to the driver side of my MG.

"Really, AJ? Couldn't you have blinked when I went by? It's early. No one's on the road now."

"I need to talk to you, Dani."

"Talk? About what?" I eyed him suspiciously. AJ was not one to ask for my advice... about anything.

"Maggie's surprise birthday party," he said.

I felt my eyebrows take a leap. "Are you sure she's a surprise party kind of person?"

I knew Maggie, and I had a funny suspicion that, as a bona fide control freak, a big surprise might be exactly the wrong approach. But if this was AJ's plan, I guess I'd go along with it. These two had a relationship I couldn't relate to, so what did I know?

AJ got a bit of a wicked grin on his face. "She'll probably hate it, but that's part of the fun, right?"

"Please tell me you're joking, AJ."

"I'm joking. Here's the thing. She's turning thirty, and I don't want her to hide away and sulk because she thinks she's turning into an old maid or something. This will force her to have fun."

"If you say so." I was still skeptical. "What do you want me to do? I've got less than zero time on my hands with the Best Business Award tomorrow night. I'm training Christine and Chad, and I have to figure out how to get Wilhelmina and her protest signs off the street."

He bent down to look at me face to face through the open window. "All you need to do is get her to Sea Breeze at six o'clock Sunday night. Rose, Sue Ellen, and Lily are doing everything else."

"How the heck am I going to get her to come with *me* on her birthday? She'll be expecting to do something with *you*."

"I've already thought of everything. I told her I have to work Sunday night. Boy, did that upset her. So, she'll be dying to go out with you girls and drown her sorrows."

He shrugged, as if working on the night of his girlfriend's big three-o birthday was something he'd just deal with another day. Men.

"Okay. I'll figure it out, but I have to get to the diner. I'm already late."

With a couple of pats on the roof of my car, he waved me on. "Try not to run Wilhelmina over. I don't think she'd appreciate that."

AJ chuckled. I never knew he had such an inappropriate sense of humor. Maybe he was beginning to lighten up a bit.

"Not funny, AJ. And you're a cop? Good thing I've known you for forever."

I put the MG in gear, spun the tires, and burnt a little rubber when they hit the tar. At least he didn't give me a ticket. Maybe, my day was improving.

Main Street through Misty Harbor was quiet this early, but a grin grew from ear to ear when I saw Luke waiting for me on the steps of the Little Dog Diner. My heart raced and with each passing day, we got closer to the wedding date we'd agreed on—Christmas Eve.

I planned to close the diner until Valentine's Day, and Luke's blueberry farm was quiet in the winter. Plus, I could look forward to a honeymoon in a nice warm spot. I wasn't sure what appealed to me the most—a warm sunny destination or leaving the fishbowl of Misty Harbor behind.

I pulled into the narrow driveway that separated the Little Dog Diner from Rose's building that housed her Blueberry Bay Grapevine weekly newspaper. Although she hadn't been spending much time there since Trouble moved in. Easier, she said, to take her old typewriter home to work so she could keep an eye on Pip's and Trouble's progress as they bonded.

"Everything's quiet this morning," Luke said as soon as I unlocked the door of the diner. "Maybe Wilhelmina will get a jump on the weekend and enjoy herself for a change, instead of harassing all the businesses on Main Street."

"Wishful thinking, I said, turning on the lights. "She never shows up until the diner is bustling with customers. She needs an audience for her flyers and propaganda about how evil we all are."

No, Wilhelmina Joy was not high on my list of favorite people. As a matter of fact, she might be smack on the bottom, just below the other business owners in town who grumbled that the Little Dog Diner received special treatment to be considered for the Best Business Award. I'd told the other three finalists, all men, that they'd better learn how to lose gracefully. It didn't go over well.

Luke helped me with the morning preparations. He made sure all the booths were clean and filled the necessary condiments. I heated the griddle and made a plate of pancakes for him. Christine and Chad would arrive soon, but this was our time, when Luke and I could do our routine without even needing to communicate.

"Have you made a decision about Wilhelmina?" Luke asked. I knew he didn't want me to try and persuade her to stop her protest. He thought it would only make her dig in and become more vocal.

He might have a point, but I had to try to stop her. My business was at stake.

"I'm going to talk to her as soon as I'm done here. Chad and Christine will do the cleanup so I can leave as soon as we put up the *CLOSED* sign."

"Want me to come with you? You know, just for moral support."

"No. I'll have Pip and some pumpkin spice muffins. If that doesn't work, nothing will."

"Oh, I forgot about your unique method of bribery." Luke grinned as I approached with a plate of pancakes.

Two could play at this teasing game and I held the pancakes out of his reach. "Hey," he said. "You know I meant that in the best possible way. Your delicious bribes always work on me."

I laughed as he licked his lips and slid the plate of pancakes in front of him. "I'm not optimistic my technique will work with Ms. Joy, but I'm still going to try."

What's the worst that could happen?

3

---

*T*he Little Dog Diner buzzed with activity by mid-morning. When three of Misty Harbor's small business owners walked in the door, I suspected something was up from the stern glances they shot in my direction. I took off my apron and joined them at their booth, hoping to head off a scene with my competitors for the Best Business Award.

"Gentlemen?" I said, nodding to each person. John Harmon owned a souvenir shop called Hidden Treasures. Larry Sidwell owned the Blueberry Bay and Beyond Tour Company. And Brent Hiller, Josie's husband, owned the Savory Soup & Sandwich Café down the street from me.

"Dani," Brent said with a forceful hiss of air.

"What are you going to do about *her*? She's already out there."

He nodded toward the street where Wilhelmina Joy marched back and forth in front of the Little Dog Diner with her protest sign. Her dog, Misty, plodded right along with her.

I didn't have to hear what she was saying because it never changed. "*Save our seas, ban single use please.*"

Her long gray ponytail danced back and forth every time she stopped and turned around. She held her sign in one hand and a pile of leaflets in the other, which she shoved at anyone who walked nearby. Most people took a wide detour around her. I'd once asked her about all the paper she wasted with her fliers, but she only glared at me.

"Should we serve her something that will put her out of her misery?" John asked. "You know, since you're the frontrunner, you could give her a free bowl of week-old clam chowder. That would send her right to the ER for a few days."

He smirked at the thought of ridding himself of Wilhelmina *plus* me once it was discovered where the chowder came from.

"Funny, John," I said without even a hint of a

smile. "I'm going to talk to her later today. She's a reasonable person, I hope."

I could hope, right? The only problem was that I suspected hope wasn't going to cut it with Wilhelmina. We'd just have to ignore her if my pumpkin spice muffins and Pip's charm didn't warm her enough to stay on her boat for the weekend instead of harassing people in town. I was sure she expected to benefit from the extra press generated by the busy weekend. She'd overshadow us, no doubt.

"At least she's moved away from my Savory Soup & Sandwich Café. Wilhelmina had a huge impact on my business, and, to be honest with you folks, I may never recover," Brent mumbled. "I wouldn't mind if that ornery neighbor of hers wrung her neck one of these days. Or maybe, she could just trip and fall into Blueberry Bay when she jumps onto her boat. Hitting her head on the way into the water would be an added benefit."

"What are you talking about?" I asked Brent. "What neighbor? She stays on her boat."

"Marcus Willoby is her boat neighbor at the Misty Marina. He splits his time between his house in Glendale and his boat here. He's closing up his boat at the end of the month, though, so I suppose if he has tolerated her for this long, he'll just stick in his earplugs and give her a rude gesture." Brent ran his hands through his hair, making it stick out in all different directions.

Something had to be done about Wilhelmina and her crusade before the small businesses in Misty Harbor felt a bigger impact, including the Little Dog Diner. I grudgingly agreed that banning single use items would help clean up Blueberry Bay, but how would a business like the Savory Soup & Sandwich Café survive with mostly take-out customers? There had to be a solution that would help the bay without hurting our businesses.

"Danielle," Larry said, "I've registered a complaint with the Best Business Award committee, just so you know. It is *my* opinion that since your grandmother is a sponsor, it gives you an unfair advantage. The committee should disqualify you for consideration for the award."

Larry hadn't touched his coffee or muffin. Did he think I was planning to poison him to end his constant complaining? Or, gain an advantage with one less competitor? The guy was a walking whining machine. He complained about everyone in town, so I didn't pay much attention to this comment. Besides, it wasn't up to us to tell the committee who to pick.

To be honest? I couldn't wait for this whole weekend to end so I didn't have to bite my tongue and be polite to Larry.

"Is that the way you gain friends and influence people to win the award Leapin' Larry?" I chuckled to myself as I walked away from that group. This annoying person would eat his words come eight o'clock Friday night when the organizers gave me a pat on my back and a "Well-done, Danielle Rose Mackenzie."

"What did you call me?"

I froze on my way back to the kitchen. Oops. Apparently, I'd said my nickname for him out loud. Brent and John snorted.

"I said, take a leap, Larry." I didn't wait around for any more questions. A line had formed at the cash register, saving me from additional embarrassment.

Between showing Chad how to get up to speed at the grill and helping Christy serve customers, the rest of the day zipped by in a blur. When I put the *CLOSED* sign in place, I sighed with relief that I could put this part of my day behind me. Although, the next part wasn't anything I looked forward to.

Rose arrived with Pip adorned in her latest bandana fashion—something she called blue wave. Whatever, Pip looked adorable. Rose took one look at me, twisted her lips to the side and asked, "What are you planning now?"

I put on my best innocent face to buy a little time. "Nothing," I answered.

"You wanted me to bring Pip here, which means you aren't heading back to Sea Breeze soon. Danielle, what's up?"

I slid onto one of the counter stools and propped my elbows on the counter. I should know by now that I couldn't hide anything from Rose. "It's Wilhelmina."

Rose, Christy, Chad, and I turned to look at the old lady as she marched to her car and stuffed her sign in the back seat. She had to leave the window down, so the pointed end protruded like a weapon. Apparently, she felt no need to protest now that we'd closed the diner for the day.

"I have to do *something* before she destroys the Little Dog Diner like she's practically done to Brent's Savory Soup & Sandwich Cafe."

Rose, next to me, said, "Okay. What's your plan?"

"I'm going to visit her at her boat and talk to her.

That's all."

"No goodies?"

"Oh, of *course* goodies will be involved." I held up a bag of muffins. "I'm hoping she has a sweet tooth *and* a soft spot for all canines which makes Pip the perfect ambassador to appeal to that side of her personality."

Rose drummed her fingers on the counter. "Should I come with you? You know, old-lady-to-old-lady kind of thing? Appeal to her maternal side? If she has one."

"No thanks. I need to do this myself instead of arriving like a huge invasion of her space. Too many people might get her hackles up. My plan is simple: make a friendly visit and explain how much I love her mission, but maybe destroying the small businesses at the same time might not be the best course to take."

"Okay. Do it your way and when that fails, I'll tell her to cease and desist before she finds her boat at the bottom of Blueberry Bay."

"You wouldn't." I was appalled by Rose's implied threat.

Rose gave me her you-never-know-what-I'm-capable-of-doing look before she laughed and patted my hand.

"I won't do anything illegal. Stop your fretting. I haven't managed to live to this ripe old age by being foolish."

"Ha. When did you learn that lesson? Yesterday?" I asked.

"Now, don't be sassy to your grandmother, Danielle. You aren't too old to be sent to your room."

I raised my eyebrows and gave her my own now-you're-just-being-ridiculous look before we both burst out laughing. I loved our back and forth banter.

"Wilhelmina is a tough old bird and means well. But she's angered just about every business here in Misty Harbor. I'm worried that she's right at the edge of someone doing something to stop her." Rose said. "Good luck."

"It doesn't have anything to do with luck, Rose. It's all about my Mackenzie charm."

I slipped off the stool, puffed up my mass of auburn curls, smiled, and fluttered my eyelashes at her. "Come on, Pip. We have a job to do."

I left the diner with my muffins, my sidekick, and a big knot in my stomach.

How would this end?

4
_____

*P*ip jumped into the MG, put her front paws on the dash and looked at me with her, can't-wait-for-the-next-adventure, tongue hanging out expression. I rubbed her head and smiled at her enthusiasm. I couldn't ask for a better companion.

I pulled onto Main Street and told Pip, "Here's the plan. Make friends with Wilhelmina's dog. That shouldn't be hard since, from what I've seen while she's doing her protest routine, Misty is cool, calm, and patient. A true gem, and Wilhelmina is lucky to have her."

Pip wagged her stubby tail and gave me a hearty yip, which had to mean she was looking forward to the agenda.

The Misty Marina, small by Misty Harbor standards, had only a handful of docks. The boats served as convenient alternatives to motels when their owners made their weekend visits. Wilhelmina was an exception. She lived on her boat for the whole season, which for her, meant May through October, or longer if the weather permitted.

I pulled into the parking lot, surprised to see a fairly quiet scene for a late Thursday afternoon. Usually, many weekenders arrived about now to let down their hair and relax. Maybe the timing was better this way. Fewer distractions.

Armed with my bribe and buddy, we walked to the end of the dock where Wilhelmina moored her boat. Her neighbor had his radio blasting, and I heard the ding of what sounded like a microwave. I bet Wilhelmina had them on her forbidden list— loud music and a microwave.

I couldn't help but wonder what he thought of *his* neighbor.

Wilhelmina's boat, named Underdog, bobbed between the pilings bordering her slip. Is that how she saw herself… as an underdog? One look at the stern and the closed door and I realized I didn't know the first thing about boat etiquette. Should I step aboard and knock?

Pip solved my problem, of course. She jumped on board and scratched on the door. Probably not the proper etiquette, but it got results. The door opened revealing a scowling face. Not a great introduction.

"What do you want?" Wilhelmina glared at me and then she looked down at Pip, and her face softened. Slightly. "Who are you?"

Pip wiggled inside without waiting for an invitation, leaving me in the awkward position of an unwanted intruder. I dove right in without letting myself worry about consequences.

"Wilhelmina?" I held out the bag of muffins. "I'm Danielle Mackenzie, and I brought you something from the Little Dog Diner. Could I come in for a minute?"

"I know who you are. I was talking to your dog." She looked at the bag, then at me, her eyes slitted with suspicion. My stomach churned. With Pip inside, it was too late to walk away and abandon my strategy. I stepped onto the back of her boat.

A loud laugh made me turn my head in the direction of her boat neighbor. Marcus Willoby, perched on his chair with his feet balanced on the railing of his boat, with what looked like a bowl of popcorn, seemed to have settled in to enjoy the show.

I ignored him and took another step toward Wilhelmina, determined to make the most of this opportunity.

She pulled the door all the way open. "Might as well come in and join your dog." She glared at Marcus. "No sense in providing *him* with any fodder for his blog at my expense."

I wondered what that was all about, but I had other fish to fry at the moment. "Thank you, Wilhelmina," I said in my friendliest tone. What did Rose always tell me? Kill them with kindness, and if that didn't work, try a bribe or something equally nefarious.

I entered her cozy cabin that had everything anyone would need in a small space—sitting area around a table opposite a sink, counter, two burners, and a bed tucked in front under the bow of the boat —definitely neat and tidy.

Pip sat quietly while Misty sniffed her nose with her tail wagging a mile a minute. "Pip and Misty seem to have hit it off," I said, hoping my comment would help to break the ice. "I brought you muffins."

Wilhelmina accepted the bag, opened it and

looked inside. "I hope they aren't loaded with a ton of sugar. Sugar's bad for you, you know. If that doesn't kill you, all the trash going into the harbor will."

"About that, Wilhelmina." It was now or never for my agenda. "You have an important cause but—"

"But? There aren't any buts. All the single serve crap you people," I guess she was referring to me in that group, "send out with your customers is choking the sea life. I spend every morning walking the shoreline picking up plastic spoons, soggy bowls, and squished plastic bottles."

She put her face right into mine. "It has to stop."

"You're right." What else could I say? "But you're also harming Misty Harbor's businesses. What about that?"

She waved her hand dismissively. "Every one of you people from restaurant owners to souvenir shops to that horrible person who takes people out to sightsee need to be closed down for good. *That* will cut down on the throw away crap. So," she shrugged, "I couldn't care less." She pulled her door open. "Now, take your dog and get out," she yelled with her finger pointed to the open door. I had no option but to retreat.

I was speechless at her rudeness. I expected I'd have a difficult time persuading her to stop her campaign, but I never expected such a completely close-minded response.

"Come on Pip." I grabbed the bag of muffins away from Wilhelmina's bird-like clutch and left her boat, slamming the door behind me. Silly, I know, but it did make me feel a little bit better to release my anger on the door.

A loud chuckle came from the boat neighbor. I looked at Marcus. Was he laughing at me? I swallowed my pride and decided that maybe he'd have some kind of suggestion to break through to Wilhelmina's better side. The compassionate side. If it existed.

"Didn't go too well, I guess," he said to me as I stopped on the dock at the end of his boat. "I see you still have your little bag of goodies. Was she afraid to eat your offering?"

"Would you like these pumpkin spice muffins, Marcus?" No sense in letting my bribe go to waste.

He flopped his bare feet off the railing, stood and flung his arm to one side, a dramatic gesture for me to board his boat. "I never say no to a pretty lady, especially if said lady is bearing a delectable gift."

Pip and I jumped across the small gap between the dock and his boat. "What can you tell me about your neighbor?"

"Sit down. Make yourself comfortable. I'm sure Wilhelmina didn't offer you a chair, did she? No need to answer. She's a grouchy old lady who seems to hate everyone. Me included." He sat down after I did. "What can I tell you? Not much, except she'd love to have me out of her life."

"Because of your blog?" I was fishing here but there was something in the way Wilhelmina had spit out the word that made me suspect it was a sore point between them.

"That, my music and this, too." He picked up what looked like a homemade cigarette. "I offered to share with her, but she threatened to call the police."

Then it dawned on me. Marcus held up a joint. "I smoke weed for my medical condition and told Miss Hoity Toity that it would help with her anger and anxiety. You know… mellow her a bit? Not surprisingly, she didn't take me up on my kind offer."

"Do you think she'd ever… do something to you?" I wondered what Wilhelmina might be capable of to get someone out of her life.

Marcus laughed and slapped his thigh. I

wondered if all the laughing and chatter was an effect of his marijuana habit. "Wilhelmina? Naw. She's harmless. All talk. I like to get under her skin."

He leaned forward in his chair so quickly, I backed away thinking he might lose his balance and crash right on top of me.

"It's great for my blog. But I'm afraid she's catching on and isn't responding so much anymore. Such a shame. My readers love my stories about my cranky, save the world, boat neighbor."

Marcus settled back in his chair and looked up at the stars. "Such a shame," he mumbled again.

"Well, thanks, Marcus." I wasn't sure what I was thanking him for, but I couldn't get away from these two people fast enough.

"Good luck with tomorrow night. I'm rooting for you to win the Best Business Award, Danielle."

"Really? Why?"

"You've got the best chowder around, and I'd hate it if Wilhelmina's protest forced you to shut down. And, there's a good story for my blog in all this somewhere. Probably about how the female prevailed in the final four and won despite the street protests and grumbling from her male competitors."

Like I wondered earlier, would this weekend drama ever end?

5

*P*ip stuck her nose in my face bright and early Friday morning. Who needed an alarm clock when I had terrier breath waking me up? Yuk.

Me? I pulled my pillow over my head with the hope of sleeping through this day. I dreaded what was coming before my eyes were even open or my feet had hit the floor.

"Okay. Okay," I said to Pip who wouldn't take no for an answer. She burrowed right under my pillow and gave me a lick from chin to forehead. "Ewww."

She knew how to get what she wanted.

I pulled on my running gear and followed her

down the stairs. Pip wasn't going to let my problems interfere with our routine.

First things first. "Morning, Rose," I said when we entered the living room. "And, Trouble," I added quickly so our new family member didn't feel left out. "We'll be back soon."

"Wait," Rose said, stopping me with a wave of her coffee mug. "How'd it go with Wilhelmina?" I hadn't seen Rose when I got home the night before. She lived and breathed early to bed and early to rise.

"Worse than I expected. She kicked us out. Can you believe it? Neither the muffins nor Pip made a dent in that granite face. But I took my muffins back so at least they didn't get wasted on her. She probably would have fed them to the seagulls just to spite me."

Rose's lips twitched at the edges. "Oh? And where are they now? Did you gobble them all up to soothe your frustration?"

"Nope. I had a chat with her boat neighbor, Marcus Willoby. He's a strange one."

I rested one knee on the arm of the couch, getting a hiss from Trouble warning me to keep my distance, I guessed. "Did you know he has a blog and writes about Wilhelmina? He says his readers love the confrontations he shares with them. I'm pretty sure Wilhelmina is *not* a fan."

"Probably not," Rose said, laughing now.

"He said he's rooting for me to survive her protests and win the business award. He thinks it'll make a good story for his blog."

"Don't knock the exposure. It could bring in new customers." Rose sipped her coffee without stopping her rhythmic stroking of Trouble who purred contentedly.

"Yeah, a bunch of aging hippies with the munchies." I headed toward the patio door, not waiting to see if her snort made her coffee spurt out her nose. "Come on Pip. Time for our run so I can get to the diner bright and early."

I did a few stretches on the patio and raced down the steps. It felt like I was in a cold, wet cloud. The only way to keep from shivering, was to try and catch up with Pip. With the sound of waves crashing on the beach as my timer, the sand gave way under my running shoes, as, stride after stride, I tried to catch up to Pip barking ahead. I hoped she was only trying to tell me the way.

I caught her at the rocky outcropping below the lighthouse and without stopping for a breather, we raced back toward Sea Breeze with me hot on Pip's heels. This time, she let me keep up with her. I guess she wanted to be sure I didn't get lost.

"Thanks, Pip," I said between gasps of air when we returned to Sea Breeze. "How would you like to hang out at the diner this morning?"

She danced a happy circle before she sat and stared at me. "You'll have to stay in my office."

It sure looked like she was smiling, so I took it to mean this plan suited her just dandy.

After a quick shower, I found clean jeans, a long-sleeved t-shirt, and tamed my curls into a messy bun. Well, at least most of my curls managed to stay in the elastic. I was good to go.

"We're off, Rose," I said, looping my bag over my shoulder. "Pip's hanging out with me."

"I'll be in before you open and bring her with me to my office."

"Perfect."

Pip took her spot in the MG, ready for whatever came along. "I see that Rose found you a new bandana—pink with bowls of steaming chowder."

I had to laugh at the creative and stylish attire Rose found for this amazing dog. "I know *you* are always rooting for me, right Pipster?"

She barked in agreement.

"And we're off."

I zipped into town, ninety-nine percent certain that no one was checking my speed this early. I pulled into the narrow driveway next to the Little Dog Diner, and took a deep breath, wondering how the day would go.

Pip jumped out, but instead of following me to the diner door, she streaked across the street. What the heck was she up to? Of course, I followed.

I lost sight of her for a minute, but her high-pitched barking led me right to the Savory Soup & Sandwich Café.

The scenario that faced me, made my stomach turn upside down.

The café door hung half off its hinges and the front serving window was smashed. Someone had vandalized Brent's business? I immediately suspected Wilhelmina, assuming her tactics had finally escalated out of control. Pip raced to my side, turned around, and disappeared behind the small building. I followed.

Misty, Wilhelmina's black lab mix, sat cowering in a corner. She gave a half-hearted bark when I appeared. Was she asking for help or defending her person? I looked around but saw no trace of Wilhelmina. Odd, because the two were normally inseparable.

I crouched next to Misty, running my hands gently over her body, checking for injuries. Nothing that I could find, but she trembled under my hands. "What's wrong, Misty?" Pip licked her.

I pulled out my phone to call Wilhelmina but realized I didn't have her phone number. Why would I? Darn. I'd have to wait for her to show up with her stupid protest sign. But I wondered again why Misty was here alone?

I couldn't explain why, but a cold sweat broke out on my body as my adrenaline surged.

With slow quiet steps, I moved to the broken door of the Savory Soup & Sandwich Café. Was someone waiting inside? My heart pounded as I peeked around the loose door. I gasped and clutched the broken door to support my wobbly legs. It couldn't be... but it was... Wilhelmina on the floor, face down, with the pointed end of her protest sign planted in her back.

Frozen in place, unable to move away from the horrible scene, I heard clomp, clomp, clomp, of boots approaching behind me.

What disaster had I run straight into?

I reached for my companion.

"Pip?" I said breathlessly as she leaned against me, providing some comfort.

"Dani?"

I let my breath out in a big woosh.

"AJ?" Relief flooded through my body. I pointed into the café. "I think someone murdered Wilhelmina."

"We just got a call from a passerby reporting vandalism at the Savory Soup & Sandwich Café. What are *you* doing here?"

Was that a tone of suspicion from AJ that *I* was the criminal?

"Pip led me here after I parked at the diner. She jumped out of my MG and ran straight here. I guess she heard something or sensed something. I don't know. Anyway, I followed and found Wilhelmina's dog, Misty, behind the cafe. What do you think happened, AJ?"

"I don't know, but Brent has some questions to answer as soon as I can find him."

"He wouldn't trash his own place," I said. Was AJ blind to all the chaos inside?

AJ backed me away from the scene and closed the door as best as he could. "You should leave. I'll find you at the diner later."

That was a relief. "What about Misty?" I pointed to the poor dog, still hiding in the corner behind Brent's cafe.

"What about her?"

"Should I take her?"

AJ looked at her. "Yes. Do you mind? Otherwise, I have to call animal control."

"That won't be necessary. I'll take her." Animal control? Was he serious? Pip and I approached the dog. I stroked her head and talked softly.

"Come on, Misty." I wasn't sure if she'd leave without Wilhelmina. She was glued to this spot.

With her dark brown eyes searching my face, she stood up and followed us back to the diner. I got the dogs settled and called Rose. "There's a big problem," I said when she answered. "Come to the diner as soon as you can."

"What happened?" Rose asked, her voice filled with panic.

"Pip and I are fine. I'll tell you the details when you get here."

I hung up, not wanting to have this discussion until she arrived.

I looked at the two dogs sitting and staring at me.

One of them knew more than she could tell me.

The other one tried her hardest to be a comforting presence.

6

*M*isty followed Pip straight into my office in the back of the Little Dog Diner. She sat on Pip's dog bed just staring at me. I wished I could read her mind. All I could imagine was that Wilhelmina, with Misty at her side, went to the Savory Soup & Sandwich Café sometime after I'd spoken to her yesterday late afternoon.

Why?

Was she meeting someone? Or, more likely, trying to confiscate all the single use items in the café so Brent couldn't serve his customers. It was obvious that someone didn't like whatever it was she'd been up to. Had Brent found her trashing his café?

The side door opened and closed. Pip dashed out of the office to see who'd entered.

"Dani? Now, tell me what's going on. I saw police vehicles and every volunteer from Misty Harbor parked around the Savory Soup & Sandwich Café. Please tell me that you aren't involved in—"

Misty followed me out of the office, effectively rendering Rose speechless when her mouth dropped open. She finally managed to ask, "Is that Wilhelmina's dog, Misty?"

"Yes, Rose."

"Don't tell me something happened to her?" Rose's eyes narrowed to slits. "You didn't do anything, did you, Danielle? I know you talked to her yesterday, and you said she kicked you off her boat. But, why do you have her dog? Is this some new strategy you've concocted? Use Misty as ransom to get her to end her protesting?"

I knew there was no point in interrupting Rose's train of thought so I waited for her questions to end. "Actually, your ransom idea would be so much better than reality."

"I don't like the sound of that." Rose walked to the front window and scanned the street. "If you have Misty and it's not for ransom, is Wilhelmina injured?"

"She's dead, Rose. Someone murdered her."

"Murdered her? Are you serious? That's terrible. I know she was difficult, but that's not a capital crime."

"The Savory Soup & Sandwich Café was also vandalized."

Rose looked a little pale. But news of a murder will do that to a person.

"Slow down, Dani," she said. "I'm confused. What do Wilhelmina and the café have in common?"

"That's where she was murdered."

"While she was destroying it?"

"I don't know, but the more I think about it, destroying property like that doesn't seem like her modus operandi. Why would she do that when she was having success hurting Brent's business with her protest? I have to wonder if someone trashed the café to make it look like she was inside and up to no good."

Rose sat on one of the counter stools as if her legs could no longer support her, shaking her head in disbelief. "Maybe someone broke in to steal something. Was anything missing?"

"How should *I* know? That's for Brent to figure out." I looked around Rose to look though the big window overlooking the street. "And there he is."

We stood shoulder to shoulder, watching as Brent pushed a police officer out of his way and ran to the door of his café. AJ blocked the open door and took Brent by his arms, leading him off to one side. I sure wished I could hear *that* conversation. Then, AJ pointed to the Little Dog Diner. I pulled Rose away from the window.

"Did you see that?" I asked Rose. "AJ just pointed this way."

"Yup. And here comes Brent. He looks like he's ready to kill someone. Quick, get out there and head him off."

"What?" Rose's suggestion floored me. "I don't know what AJ told Brent. He might have said I was at the scene of the crime and now you're sending me to intercept a furious person with a possible murderous intent?"

"That was just a figure of speech." Rose pushed me to the door.

As much as I would rather just lock us inside, I walked outside to meet Brent and try to calm him down. Of course, I had Pip at my side for protection if needed. She was small but she could launch herself like a surprise missile attack when necessary. "Brent."

"Dani? What did you do to my café? AJ said he found you there." He leaned down to my eye level. His coffee breath enveloped me to the point of making me nauseous.

"You vandalized my café to get rid of your competition in town?" He spit right next to my foot.

At least he missed me, but Pip growled a warning.

I poked Brent in his chest hoping he'd back up out of my personal space. He didn't budge. His chest was as broad and hard as a cement wall.

"You listen to me, Brent. You're accusing *me* of trashing your café? Think before you embarrass yourself with any more stupid words falling out of your mouth." I backed up so he wasn't towering right over me. "Where were *you* last night?"

His eyes might as well have turned red with the rage on his face.

"You think *I* did all that to my own business?"

"That's not what I said. But that's what Detective AJ Crenshaw will be asking you if he hasn't already. I hope you have an alibi, that's all I'm saying."

"I was sleeping." All his bluster was gone. "Josie

was working all night at the station, and she got the call about the vandalism. She called me, but I guess I didn't hear it ring, so she left a message."

He ran his fingers through his hair like he was trying to find some kind of alibi there.

"Come on inside, Brent." I took his arm. "I'll fix up some coffee if you want any."

I truly felt sorry for him. I knew what he was going through with his café destroyed since I'd been through something similar. Was this town a magnet for restaurant murders?

Rose already had a selection of muffins, tea, and coffee waiting on the counter. "Brent, help yourself while we figure out who might have wanted Wilhelmina dead."

Rose slid onto one of the stools and patted the one next to her.

Brent, frozen in place, said, "Dead? What are you talking about?"

I looked at Rose. Apparently, AJ hadn't told Brent about that, not so minor, detail. Oh boy. Thanks a lot, AJ. I couldn't believe he sent Brent over knowing I might drop that bombshell on this unsuspecting person.

As if we didn't have enough company, the side door opened, and Maggie Marshall, Misty Harbor's exceptional—and   only—   private   investigator, walked inside. She rubbed her eyes and had the worst case of bed head I'd ever seen. "I know you aren't open for business yet, but I need coffee."

Maggie rented the apartment next door, over the Blueberry Bay Grapevine, Rose's weekly paper. The other important detail about Maggie was that she had her sights on Detective Crenshaw. As a matter of fact, he was the reason she relocated to Misty Harbor.

They had a few details in their personal relationship to work out. The biggest one being how she always managed to weasel her way into every investigation. That didn't work for AJ. At all.

I saw a big problem looming up once she heard about Wilhelmina.

"Hey, Brent," Maggie said as she slid onto the stool next to him. "What brings you here so bright and early?"

"Maggie," I said, "did you happen to notice any activity on Main Street this morning?"

"Nope. I stumbled down the stairs, walked across the driveway, and," she spread her arms out, "here I am. Why, what's up?"

"Murder," I said.

What was the point of beating around the bush?

7

---

*M*aggie stared at me with her eyes blinking out some kind of Morse code. Or, at least that's what it looked like after I'd uttered the word *murder*.

She shook her head, then tapped one side with the heel of her hand. "What did you say? I guess I'm in more desperate need of that coffee than I thought. There's something wrong with my hearing this morning."

Brent sat, unmoving, with his head resting on his arms, folded on the counter.

Rose got another mug and set it in front of Maggie. "Help yourself to the coffee and there's nothing wrong with your hearing. Somebody murdered Wilhelmina in the Savory Soup & Sandwich Café sometime last night or early this morning. Dani has her dog, Misty, here with us."

"That's all we know," I said. Except the minor detail of Wilhelmina's sign piercing her body. I wished I could get that image out of my memory bank.

And that summed up my morning. Just another day in the life of Danielle Mackenzie — chaos.

I helped myself to tea. Coffee? Not a big fan if I had a choice. The muffins tempted me, too. Maggie had moved off to the far end of the diner. It wasn't hard to figure out that she was talking to AJ. Not that he'd give her any details, but the lure of a murder investigation was like catnip to Ms. Maggie Marshall, PI.

Brent finally lifted his head off his arms. "Someone is setting me up. That's all I can think. Someone else, besides Wilhelmina, wants my business to fail."

His eyes pleaded with me to give him an explanation that made sense, that he could wrap his head around.

I studied Brent while he slumped on the stool. Was he a great actor or was he a murderer?

"Maybe," I said, "someone was out to get Wilhelmina. They followed her, saw the perfect opportunity to get rid of her, and she just happened to be in your café. That could describe any number of people in Misty Harbor in my opinion, since she'd alienated just about everyone here. But that doesn't explain *why* she was in your café, Brent."

Before I could come up with any more theories, AJ banged on the front door of the diner. Great, I thought. Now, there'd be fireworks between Maggie and AJ on top of dealing with Brent. *And* I still needed to get the diner ready to open on time.

Just like I imagined when I woke up—nothing but trouble today. Although, I never imagined murder would be on the menu.

Rose opened the door for AJ. Might as well open for business, anyway. With all the commotion outside, there wouldn't be a shortage of customers coming in hoping to pick up a bit of gossip about Wilhelmina. I doubted there'd be a shortage of theories, either.

"Brent? Come with me, please. I want you to look and see if anything is missing from your café." Maggie jumped up to follow behind AJ. "Just Brent," he said.

Maggie stopped, liked she'd been slapped by his words. She sagged into one of the booths and stared out the window. I really didn't have time to cheer her up with customers about to arrive, but she was my friend and needed a shoulder to cry on. I'd give her two and a half minutes to get her act together.

Fortunately, Christy and Chad arrived. Chad headed straight to the grill and began to organize the pancake batter, eggs, and bacon. Christy found the muffins I'd set out to thaw and slid the trays into the glass display. They were learning quickly and fitting in well.

"Maggie," I said, "AJ has a job to do. You can't take his rebukes so hard."

"I know, but it's easier said than done. My care-taking side business I use to fill my down time just doesn't have the same adrenaline rush that searching a crime scene for clues has. And I'm *good* at investigating." She lifted her head and looked at me. "Do you think Brent might hire me?"

I shrugged, not wanting to put words in someone else's mouth. "I don't know if he can even afford you, to be honest."

The door jingled. I had to get to work, but before I slid out of the booth, Brent's wife, Josie slid in next to me, blocking my exit.

"I got to Brent's café as soon as my shift ended, but he sent me over here to find you, Maggie. We need to hire you to find out what happened. Brent wants to head this problem off as soon as possible before he completely loses his business. Between Wilhelmina's harassment, and now the vandalism," she brushed what looked like tears off her cheeks, "we'll have a lot of bills and only my income as the 9-1-1 dispatcher."

Maggie looked at me with her eyebrows raised. I guessed she wanted to know what I thought she should say. I nodded back letting her know how lucky she was with this wish-fulfilling request.

"I'll do it, and we'll figure out a payment plan you can live with, Josie."

"It might be soup and a sandwich for life," Josie said. She lifted her palms up to indicate that's about all she had to offer at the moment.

"Sounds perfect to me since I don't cook. A girl's gotta eat. Let's go and find Brent; see if AJ will let us inside. I want to get a look around."

I was glad that Maggie's enthusiasm was back and her turn around took less than the two and a half minutes I'd allotted. I gave myself a pat on my back, even if it was all Josie's doing.

Great. Now, I could focus on feeding my customers who would be trickling in anytime soon and then get myself mentally prepared for the award ceremony tonight.

Unfortunately, Rose slid in opposite me before I managed to get my butt in gear. She didn't say anything, just tilted her head and raised an eyebrow, which was her way of letting me know that she was waiting to hear *my* thoughts.

"Do you think the vandalism is connected to the murder?" I asked her.

"It's too early to know. Why, what are you thinking?"

"I'm thinking there are two possibilities. One, the murder was completely random."

"And, your second theory?"

"The vandalism and the murder are connected. But neither one explains why Wilhelmina was in the café to begin with."

"There could be a third possibility," Rose said. "Would Brent, Larry, or John benefit from sensationalizing the Best of Blueberry Bay Weekend? Bring in more curious tourists and get rid of Wilhelmina's protesting. Think about it, Dani. Brent's business was already suffering, and I don't think it was all Wilhelmina's fault. She was more of a nuisance than anything else. Larry has spent heavily promoting his boat tours for this weekend, and John sells all those cheap lighthouse and lobster

Maine souvenirs that Wilhelmina hated since most of his stuff is made in China."

"You think one of them planned a murder to benefit their business?"

I felt sick to my stomach. Wilhelmina wasn't a fan of mine but this theory for a murder was beyond despicable.

"All three of those men were upset that you're the frontrunner to win the Misty Harbor Best Business Award tonight. Why wouldn't they try something to help sabotage your success?"

"If the goal was to attract more tourists to town, that would help all of us, not just this possible murderer," I said.

"It won't help Brent since his café is destroyed."

"Which eliminates him as the murderer?" I asked.

"Possibly. I think it helps Larry or John the most. Larry counts on selling out his tours, and I heard John brag that he'd ordered double what he usually handles. They can't afford to lose business because of Wilhelmina's protests."

"Do you think that whoever is behind what happened has something else planned?" I asked Rose.

"That thought has crossed my mind. You need to be extra careful."

"You think I could be the next target?"

"I didn't say that. Brent wasn't murdered, just traumatized. This killer might have a cunning plan to mislead us all into thinking only about *who* killed Wilhelmina with the hope that no one thinks there's a link to the Best of Blueberry Bay Weekend.

If that was the plan, would anyone be able to stop it?

8

---

*T*he bell above the door of the Little Dog Diner jingled. A sound that usually inspired me into action, but this morning, I felt more like I was sleepwalking through a familiar routine.

Until I looked up to see Marcus Willoby, sitting on a stool at the counter. He folded his paper and tucked it down by his feet. "Orange juice, egg sandwich on whole wheat, and a strong coffee, please."

I jotted his order on my pad and slid it through the window to Chad before I returned with his orange juice and the coffee pot. "Black?"

"Definitely. I had to drive to my house to pick up some papers I forgot to bring to my boat for the weekend but couldn't find them. Searched everywhere and now I'm doubting my sanity because they were in my car all along." He shook his head and laughed. "But I couldn't sleep, and driving is a good distraction from all the stuff going on up here." He tapped his finger on the side of his head. "The marijuana doesn't always help with my PTSD."

I poured his coffee. PTSD? "From your military service?" I asked.

"Yeah but I don't want to talk about it. Anyway, what's all the commotion over at the soup café? I had trouble finding a parking spot." He sipped his coffee.

"Vandalism and murder. I don't know what order or even if the two are connected."

I decided Marcus, as Wilhelmina's boat neighbor, might have more insight about her than most of us. "It appears that someone decided they'd had enough of your boat neighbor's protests."

Fortunately, Marcus had already swallowed his mouthful of coffee so when he choked, nothing shot out but a series of coughs and gasps. He did, however, spill half the cup's content on the saucer, which overflowed onto the counter.

"Say what?"

I leaned my elbows on the counter and lowered my voice. "You interacted with Wilhelmina probably more than anyone in Misty Harbor. Someone murdered her. Any idea who would do that?"

"Murdered? How?"

"Well, I guess that's something the police will reveal when they're ready." Sure, I'd seen the brutality of her sign sticking through her, but I wasn't going to be the leaker of that detail.

"At the soup café? Probably that owner, Brent, right? Wilhelmina was always complaining about how much waste that place generated. He was at the top of her list of businesses to shut down."

Marcus pulled out a bunch of paper napkins and soaked up the mess that had sloshed off his saucer. He looked at the soggy mess on the counter.

"She wasn't too fond of this place, either. Paper napkins? Such a waste according to Wilhelmina. Brent probably did you a favor by silencing her. My guess is that you'd be her next target if she was still around."

I couldn't believe what he was saying. "She told you that?"

"Well, not in so many words, but it wasn't hard to figure out her path of destruction. It's all on my blog—Musings in Misty Harbor—and lately it's been all about my crazy boat neighbor. I didn't use her name, of course, but all of her nutty rants made for great material to share with my followers."

This was terrible news. If AJ discovered Marcus's blog, he'd have me down as one of the suspects, too, if he didn't already. Why was I so often in the wrong place at the wrong time? I might need to hire Maggie myself.

Toenails clicking on the diner floor brought me out of my funk. Rose led Pip and Misty toward the door but not before Marcus snarled, "What's that dog doing in here?"

Misty growled and lunged, but Rose had her on a short leash. She kept the two dogs moving. "Sorry about that," she said to Marcus. "Misty went through something traumatic." To me, she added, "I'll take them both next door to my office while I'm working on this week's Blueberry Bay Grapevine."

Marcus kept watch over Misty as he turned the counter stool in Rose's direction. "Will you be writing about Wilhelmina? I'd like to be the first to blog about this latest turn of events."

"Well, my paper comes out every Friday." Rose gave me her what's-up-with-this-guy look, her mouth twisted to one side and her eyebrows creased in the middle. Before she continued to the door, she added, "I hope you don't intend to sensationalize the murder and give Misty Harbor bad press."

Christy slid Marcus's breakfast in front of him, distracting him from Rose's comment for a second or two. "Well, I have my style and you have yours Ms. Mackenzie. Isn't the goal to give our readers what they want?"

He swiveled his stool back so he faced his breakfast, tucked a napkin into the top of his t-shirt and picked up the sandwich. This effectively ended the conversation with Rose.

"I'll be over when I can," I said to her as she maneuvered the two dogs outside. I wished I were leaving with them, and maybe just driving back to the peace and quiet of Sea Breeze or to see Luke at Blueberry Acres. Now, that would be the best way to spend the day and get my mind off this mess.

"Everything, okay, Dani?" Christy whispered in my ear as she went by with a handful of orders. "If you have to leave, Chad and I can manage."

That sounded so tempting. Should I take her up on the offer?

"By the way, Dani." Marcus lifted his head from his focus on his breakfast.

What now?

"Could I interview you as one of the finalists for

the Best Business Award? It would be great free promotion for you." He used the last edge of toast to clean up a bit of egg that had fallen out of his sandwich while he waited for my answer.

Did I want his followers in the diner? That probably wasn't fair to a lot of decent people. What I especially didn't want was to encourage this person and what seemed to be his warped way of using others when they were having problems.

"I'll think about it, Marcus."

Let him wonder, even though at this point, I couldn't see any advantage for me, to sit down for an interview with this man, besides the slim possibility of a few new customers.

"Brent Hiller, Larry Sidwell, and John Harmon have already agreed to an interview. If *you* say yes, it will be four of Misty Harbor's best business owners chatting about what makes for a successful small business. Sounds great, right? Free publicity, don't forget." He slid a corner of a napkin with his phone number written on it, across the counter to me. "Call me."

"Okay," I said. It seemed like the easiest answer to get him off my back. And, taking Christy up on her offer to handle the Little Dog Diner for the rest of the day seemed like the easiest solution to my distraction.

I untied my apron, grabbed my shoulder bag, and told Christy to call me if it got too over-whelming in the diner. I also put a selection of muffins in a bag, just in case. I never knew when or for whom, a sweet offering might come in handy.

I had something on my mind at the moment, and it wasn't the award ceremony coming up tonight.

9

*R*ose turned around when I opened her office door. Silence draped the room like an awkward guest. Did I barge into a secret gathering between my grandmother and two of my best friends?

"Oh, I didn't know Sue Ellen and Lily were here with you," I said. "Am I interrupting?" It certainly felt like I was. Pip and Misty were the only ones to make me feel welcome with tails wagging and happy faces greeting me.

"No. Not at all." Rose recovered from her surprised expression quickly. "Why aren't you working? Did you close the diner?"

I guess that question explained her confusion at my entrance. "No. Christy could tell I was distracted. She'll call if it gets too busy for her and Chad to handle." I plopped onto Rose's cozy chair, crossed my legs, and waited.

Sue Ellen, dressed in red—her signature color— today in a fleece top over stylish black pants, broke the silence first. "*You* found Wilhelmina's body? You poor thing."

She pulled me out of the chair and wrapped me in her arms, which did help to transfer some of the horrible memory off my own shoulders. I even choked up a little knowing these women had my back for better or worse.

"Let's not talk about that," I said pulling myself out of Sue Ellen's embrace. "There's something more important right now. Did any of you know about Marcus Willoby's blog?"

"I came across it recently. Musings in Misty Harbor, right?" Lily asked.

I nodded. "Since when do you follow blogs, Lil?"

"Only because he mentioned the Best of Blue- berry Bay Weekend and how his boat neighbor was protesting outside the Little Dog Diner. Really, Dani, you should Google your business once in a while, so you know what's going on."

"I don't need Google when I hear everything straight from the horse's mouth," I said.

"That rude man," Rose said, disgust pasted on her face. "He's planning to use this tragedy to bring attention to himself, but I'll figure out a way to stop him."

"You didn't even hear his *latest* plan," I said. "He's got an interview scheduled for this afternoon. He asked me to participate, but I have no intention of being part of whatever he's got up his sleeve. I told him I'd think about it to put him off for a bit. Supposedly, Brent, John, and Larry are a go with Marcus. You know, free promotion, according to him."

"Ha!" Rose's outburst surprised me. "I'm not sure his followers will ever come to the Little Dog Diner. They all live on snacks and booze. Of course, I may be stereotyping because that's what I think about Marcus."

"He ate at the diner this morning," I pointed out.

"Is that the first time he ever set foot inside?" I was pretty sure Rose already knew the answer to her question.

"Yeah, I think you're right."

"Just what I thought. He came in to soften you

up with the expectation that you'd say yes to his interview. And you know what?"

We all waited for Rose to continue.

"I wouldn't be so sure he has those other three on board. He's the type that would use you all against each other."

"How do you know so much about Marcus Willoby?" I asked Rose.

Rose chewed on the corner of her lip before she answered. "Before he started this blog thing, he thought he could start a newspaper and put me out of business. He's nasty, dishonest, and I wouldn't trust him as far as I can spit."

Rose certainly didn't mince any words. And, I had to assume that those two were not big best buddies. "But we," she circled her hand to include Lily, Sue Ellen, and me, "can beat him at his own game since we're smarter than he is."

"What's his game?" Sue Ellen asked.

"Attention, I think. And, troublemaking in general. But I've got a plan."

I couldn't wait to hear Rose's plan. Something had to be done.

"I'm planning a special addition of the Blueberry Bay Grapevine to beat Marcus to the first bit of publicity about Wilhelmina. He'll be livid."

Rose chuckled at her strategy. "And I'm going to see if the organizers will postpone the awards ceremony planned for tonight. Just to give Brent a breather since he's one of the finalists for the award. I'm counting on AJ's help to put pressure on them."

I sighed with relief. I realized that most of my stress was from the combination of Wilhelmina's protest, her murder, and, I had to admit, Larry's complaint to the organizers had gotten under my skin. A breather would be good for me, too.

"So," Rose said, bringing me out of my own thoughts, "while I head over to the Savory Soup & Sandwich Café to find out what I can, you three should go to Sea Breeze and put the finishing touches on Maggie's surprise birthday party. AJ talked to you about that, didn't he, Dani?"

"He did, but all he said was that I need to get Maggie to Sea Breeze at six-fifteen Sunday night. With all this other stuff, do you think his plan is still a go?"

"Of course. We'll just have to make time for the party."

"Is there anything else I need to do?" I couldn't imagine my list getting any longer.

"Nope. But since you aren't working at the diner

today, you might as well help Lily and Sue Ellen figure out the food."

She picked up her hobo bag and headed for the door, leaving us to do whatever it was we were going to do. She focused on *her* agenda now.

I snapped the leash on Misty's collar, not wanting to risk having her run off, even though I didn't think that was much of a worry.

"I'll meet you two at Sea Breeze, but first I'm going to introduce Misty to someone."

"You aren't keeping her?" Lily asked.

"That's not what I said." I tried to keep the smile from giving me away. "But I do have a plan. I know someone who'd love a dog, and Misty is quiet, well behaved, and used to having company."

"Who?" Sue Ellen asked. "I'd consider adopting her but with all my charity work, she'd probably have to stay home alone quite a bit."

"No worries, Sue Ellen. I'm thinking that your neighbor, Alice, will be thrilled to have a sweet companion like Misty. I'll stop by and play it by ear. Are you two all set for a couple of hours before I join you?"

"Yup," Lily said. "We didn't expect you to help us today anyway so take your time."

Perfect, I thought as Pip led Sue Ellen and Lily

out of Rose's office. I followed with Misty at my side. I wasn't sure how the two dogs would fit on the front seat of my MG, but I shouldn't have worried. I couldn't believe that Pip had the sense to squeeze in the back, leaving the front seat for Misty. What a sweetheart.

As I drove down Main Street, past the Savory Soup & Sandwich Café, I saw Rose talking to AJ and Brent. Josie and Maggie were several feet away having their own conversation. I hoped Rose's plan to postpone the event worked. Postponing would be a big help, but I still had to figure out what I was going to do about Marcus Willoby and his interview.

What a pain.

10

I pulled into Alice's driveway, glad, when I exited the MG that I'd planned ahead with a bag of fresh muffins. Misty happily followed Pip, or maybe, it was the aroma oozing from the Little Dog Diner bag.

As I walked up the path to the front door, I saw Alice sitting in her chair that provided a view through her big front window. I waved and she beamed a huge smile back at me.

"Now, put on your best manners, Misty. Alice doesn't know it, but this is your tryout for a new forever home. She loves dogs, so you shouldn't have any trouble wowing her."

The door opened. "What a wonderful surprise, Danielle. And, who did you bring with you today?"

I also noticed that Alice eyed the bag I was holding but she was too well-mannered to ask about that.

Pip had already squeezed by Alice, but Misty sat at my side looking up at the two of us. "This is Misty."

"Well, it's wonderful to meet you, Misty," Alice said. "Come in and join Pip. I'm guessing she's waiting next to my chair where I keep the jar of dog treats."

Alice's assumption was spot on. Pip knew the routine even though we'd only visited a handful of times. There she was, sitting and panting. We both chuckled at Pip's memory.

I waited for Alice to get settled in her chair before I placed the bag of muffins in her lap. "These are *not* for the dogs," I pointed out.

She peeked inside with the expectation of a little kid. "Oh, Danielle, you didn't forget how your treats put a smile on this old face. First things first, though." She picked up the jar with canine treats and handed one to each dog.

"There, now I can enjoy a muffin without four eyes and two drooling faces begging and making me feel guilty."

She selected a muffin and held the bag toward me.

"No thanks. They're all for you, Alice." I sat kitty-corner to her chair, enjoying being with my friend and the two dogs enjoying their treats.

In between bites, she said, "Did you hear about Wilhelmina?"

This comment caught me by surprise. How did the news travel so quickly?

"I did. I… uh… was the first at the scene."

"Oh? How horrible!" Apparently, the gory topic didn't interfere with Alice's appetite. She stuffed the rest of the muffin in her mouth and dabbed the crumbs off the corner of her lips with an embroidered handkerchief.

"My daughter called me first thing since she knew that Wilhelmina and I were friends.

"Really? I didn't know she *had* any friends." I said. Not that I knew Wilhelmina Joy well at all, but with her nasty attitude, I couldn't imagine that she endeared herself to many people in town.

"Well, not *friends*, exactly, but I *have* known her for quite some time. She was difficult with all her protesting even if it was for a good cause. The problem was, she refused to consider the effect on others or even try to work out a more reasonable solution for the problem without destroying businesses in the process."

Alice shook her head, obviously distraught about Wilhelmina's plight.

She glanced at Misty. "Now I recognize you. This is *her* dog, isn't it? They were a team for at least ten years. Always together."

I nodded, not sure how to open the subject of Misty needing a new home.

"What will happen with her now?" Alice patted the dog and Misty put her head on the older woman's lap. "You're such a sweetheart, aren't you, Misty?"

If I didn't know better, I'd think Misty knew this was her chance for a new mistress. The two were bonding already.

"She needs a home where she can be with someone all the time," I said. "That's what she's used to, and I can't bring her to the diner when I'm working, so—"

"And, you have Pip," Alice added before I could even finish my comment. She patted Pip as if she didn't want her to feel left out.

"And Trouble, now, too."

"Trouble? What trouble is that?"

I laughed realizing her misunderstanding about Trouble being an animal and not a problem to deal with. Although, he was sort of *both*, but in a good way. "Trouble is a cat who has been living at the police station. Josie, the new dispatcher is allergic to cats, so Rose brought him to Sea Breeze."

"Well, then, you and Rose have your hands full with the animals you've already taken in. I'll keep Misty."

Alice said it casually as she leaned forward and stroked Misty's head with both of her gnarled hands.

"She's such a sweet dog. Quiet, too. She'll be great company for me."

"Are you sure?" I crossed my fingers that Alice's offer wasn't a spontaneous thought that she'd back out of after the responsibility sank in.

"Absolutely. I keep telling my daughter that I don't like living alone. Misty is mature and calm. She'll provide the peace of mind that I've been craving. Plus, it's just nice to have another living creature here to talk to. Right, Misty?"

I had to smile at Alice and Misty. They seemed the perfect pair now that I saw them together. While Alice talked, Misty listened, keeping her deep soulful eyes focused on Alice the whole time. A match made in heaven as far as I was concerned.

"What about taking her outside?" To be honest,

until just now, I hadn't even considered how Alice, with her limited mobility, would take care of Misty.

"I still have a doggie door for when I had Princess. It goes straight into the fenced-in back garden. She'll be no trouble at all. What do you think about that, Misty?" Misty thumped her tail. If I had a tail, it would be beating out some happy tune right now, too. "It's the least I can do for Wilhelmina. You know, she called me last night. If I'd known it would be the last conversation I'd ever have with her, I could have told her that I'd take Misty in if anything ever happened to her. Of course, who would have suspected this terrible tragedy?"

"She called you?" I asked. "I visited her yesterday afternoon. Did she mention that?"

"She did. And I told her she shouldn't have been so rude to you, Danielle. But Wilhelmina only listened to Wilhelmina." Alice bit into a second muffin. "She told me that she was heading into town to meet someone. I'm pretty sure she said it had something or other to do with her protest."

I scooched forward in my chair.

"Did she say who she was meeting?"

"Well," Alice looked up at nothing. "I don't remember if she did before she hung up. She was odd like that; she'd call just to tell me one thing and then hang up. It wasn't unusual for her, so I didn't really worry about it. Do you think that person she was meeting could be the murderer?"

"Could be. Is there anything else that you can remember about your conversation with her?"

Alice pursed her lips and drummed her fingers on the arm of her chair. "Oh, my goodness. Now I remember. I believe she said she was meeting someone by the name of Brent."

My heart sank to my toes.

Did Brent take matters into his own hands and kill the person he blamed for trying to put him out of business?

I stood up, not wanting to tire Alice out. "I can keep Misty with me if you need more time to think about adopting her."

"Oh, no. My mind is made up as long as Misty wants to live with me." She looked at Misty. "What do you think?" We both waited, for what, I wasn't sure, but then Misty wagged her tail. "See? She agrees." That must have been the sign Alice needed to know she'd made the right decision.

Pip and I left Misty with Alice. They both looked like they'd had enough excitement for the morning and might be settling in for a power nap.

Instead of driving to Sea Breeze to help Sue Ellen and Lily with Maggie's surprise birthday party, I headed to Blueberry Acres. If anyone could help me sort out this latest information from Alice, it would be Luke.

Pip, with her front paws on the dashboard, let me know that she was ready for a visit to the farm, too. After all, there were chipmunks to chase.

11

*P*ip ran straight to the stone wall at the side of the old farmhouse at Blueberry Acres when I opened the door of the MG. Chipmunk heaven. Of course, she never caught any because they knew each and every hiding hole among the fieldstone wall.

Pip loved the challenge, though.

I walked around to the back of the house, scanning the blueberry fields for Luke. He wasn't in sight anywhere, so I turned around to check inside.

"Yikes!" I yelped when I turned right into his strong chest. "Don't sneak up on me like that." I patted my chest in a silly attempt to slow my racing heart.

Luke chuckled. "Well, if you gave me a warning

that you decided to play hooky from work, I would have planned something special for today. Maybe a picnic somewhere quiet and secluded."

He tipped an eyebrow as he looked at me. My worried expression must have clued him into the fact that I might not just be playing hooky. "What's wrong?"

Luke put a comforting arm around my shoulders and led me into the house. "Want some mint tea?"

"That's about the best thing I've heard all day," I said as I sank into one of the kitchen chairs at the big pine farm table.

"Okay. That makes me wonder what else you've heard today since, as delicious as mint tea is, I wouldn't expect it to top my list of all the great things that I could hear before lunch." He turned on the burner under the kettle before he sat next to me.

Pip scratched at the back door. "I wonder if she managed to lower the chipmunk population today," Luke said as he opened the door.

"The stone wall gives them amazing cover. It's just a game for Pip, I hope." The kettle whistled. I filled the rose covered teapot that had been Luke's mom's favorite. "Did you hear this morning's news?"

Luke put porcelain cups that matched the teapot, on the table. "I heard geese flying over, and I saw the mama doe and her twin fawns at the edge of the blueberry field. Do you have something more interesting to tell me?"

"Unfortunately, yes." I caught Luke up to speed with the murder details that I knew so far and what I'd learned from Alice when I brought Misty to her house. He sat transfixed while I talked.

"I can't believe it. Alice told you that Wilhelmina was meeting Brent last night?"

"She thinks that's what she remembers. At any rate, it fits with the evidence—Wilhelmina was murdered in Brent's café. If he called her to meet him there, that, at least, explains *why* she was at the café." I sipped the tea letting the hot mint soothe my nerves. "And, you know what the worst part is?"

Luke waited.

"I found her because Pip ran straight to the back of the café where Misty was hiding. When I looked in the broken door, there she was, Luke. It was terrible."

He crouched next to me. My sadness finally overwhelmed me. I couldn't help sobbing uncontrollably on his shoulder when his arms wrapped tightly around me.

"And you know what else?" I hiccupped and sniffled. "Wilhelmina's boat neighbor, Marcus, has a blog chronicling all of his conversations with her. He told me she implied I'd be her next target for a protest."

"You don't have to worry about that anymore."

"Not that, but AJ found me at the scene of the crime, Luke. If Brent has an alibi, I'll be smack on top of that suspect list."

Luke rubbed my back and rested his chin on the top of my head. "You've been there before, Dani, and you survived. Besides, from what you just told me, both Misty and Pip should be above you on the list."

I pulled away so I could see his face. "You think one of the dogs picked up that sign and speared Wilhelmina with it?"

"Probably not Misty, but Pip is pretty amazing. And she can balance on her back legs."

Pip, hearing her name, perked up, but when no treats went her way, she rested her head on her paws again.

"I'll be sure to run that theory by AJ. And then he'll lock me up… to protect Misty Harbor from a whacko."

Luke chuckled. "A charming whacko. Finish your tea. We need to go to Wilhelmina's boat and get all of Misty's supplies. Don't you think Alice will need a dog bed, food bowl, and whatever food is still left?"

I knew Luke would have a brilliant idea. My tea disappeared in record time and I didn't even burn my tongue. "I hope AJ doesn't have the boat taped off already."

Luke pulled me to a standing position. "Let's go find out."

I hoped Wilhelmina left some clues on her boat that could help lead us to the killer. I didn't want to imagine that Brent killed Wilhelmina. He didn't seem the type, but who ever knew what was going on in someone else's head.

I knew *I* hadn't murdered Wilhelmina. Brent's wife Josie had the same motive as Brent—save the Savory Soup & Sandwich Café. Rose's theory about Larry and John wanting to increase tourists in town made for a motive, but strong enough to talk one of them into murder? That's what I wanted to find out, and I knew who would help me, even though he didn't know it yet.

If Marcus Willoby wanted to have an interview, I might have to rethink my decision not to sit down with him. Maybe, just maybe, an interview would lead to interesting details from the new perspective of who might have the strongest motive.

My head began to hurt with this new twist. Larry already had a complaint against me with the organizers, which, as far as I was concerned, amounted to nothing except to show his desperation. Would he try to eliminate me to help his chance of winning the Best Business Award?

That's what I had to find out.

12

I parked the MG in front of the Misty Marina office and made a mental note to talk to Kyle Johnson, the marina manager, after I got all of Misty's belongings from Wilhelmina's boat. Kyle might be able to shed more light on Wilhelmina, especially any unusual activity she was involved in or if she'd had any visitors the day before. Besides me, of course.

Pip darted down the dock. Apparently, she remembered where we'd gone yesterday. She glanced back at me as if to say, you'll thank me later for what I'm about to do. That's when I saw AJ standing on the back of Wilhelmina's boat and had a feeling that Pip would just jump aboard and disrupt their search like she'd done in the past.

Luke took my hand. "It sure looks like Pip knows your plan. Do you two have some sort of secret communication I should know about? I mean, I don't want the two of you plotting against me after we get married. You know, telling Pip to steal my favorite jeans because it's time for a wash but I want to wear them one more time. Or, curl up in the comfy chair so I'm forced to cuddle with you."

I stopped walking and looked at Luke. "*Forced* to cuddle with me? Really? I think you'll have to thank Pip for giving up that sacred spot next to me after we're married. How do you know she'll even do that? You might just get a nip if you try to squeeze between us."

"Hmmm… you did warn me that Pip was part of the package when you said yes to my proposal, but now I have to wonder if I thought it through properly."

I leaned into Luke and bumped him with my shoulder. "Thanks for making me laugh. I don't think you'll have anything to worry about. You'll have all the cuddles you want."

"That's a relief." He put his arm around my shoulder and pulled me close. "I was afraid I'd have to ask Rose to do an intervention, or something."

"Dani!" AJ's angry shout traveled down the

dock and forced me to focus on the task at hand instead of the much more interesting idea of cuddling with Luke Sinclair. Darn. "What is Pip doing on this boat?"

Searching for clues, I wanted to yell back, but of course what I said was, "Getting Misty's belongings."

When Luke and I reached the end of the dock where AJ stood with his hands fisted on his hips, he asked me in a sharp tone, "What clues?"

Oops. I couldn't believe I'd let that tidbit about clues slip out. I had to learn to keep those thoughts where they belonged. Luke nudged my side, a reminder I guessed, to be careful about what I said to AJ. Well, *that* reminder came three words too late.

"What clues?" AJ asked again but this time he acted as if he'd discovered something that I wouldn't like.

"Clues about why Wilhelmina left her boat last night to meet someone?" I tried to peek around AJ, but he wasn't having it. He moved to block my view.

"*You* came here last night, Dani. What was *that* about? According to Marcus who has his boat next to Wilhelmina's, she kicked you out." AJ leaned right in my face. "I bet that upset you. Even made you angry. You don't like it when you don't get your way."

I knew he was taunting me, but words flew out of my mouth as if they had wings. "She insulted my *muffins*. She said sugar was as bad as all the stuff that ended up in the harbor. My *muffins*, AJ. Who can reason with someone who doesn't like *muffins*?"

A smile appeared at the edges of his mouth, but not so far that it traveled to his eyes. It wasn't a happy smile, and I knew it. I had to think of something fast. I'd practically given him a reason to lock me up and throw the key away. "I went home after I talked to Wilhelmina."

"Marcus said you had a chat with him and gave *him* muffins. How many muffins were you hauling around last night?"

"I only talked to Marcus for a few minutes. Since Wilhelmina didn't want the muffins I brought for her, I gave them to Marcus. *Then* I went home."

"So, Rose can vouch for you being at Sea Breeze last night?"

"Well, she was already in her room when I got home." Was it possible for me to dig this hole any deeper?

Luke squeezed my hand. I was thankful for his support, but I wasn't happy with how badly I'd botched this conversation. Instead of finding any clues to figure out who murdered Wilhelmina, I'd stepped right into a swamp and was sinking fast.

"Listen, Dani. The fact that you were at the scene of the crime, and now you've come snooping around the victim's boat, makes me wonder what's so darn important here." AJ's glare made me squirm, but Luke, like a gallant knight, stepped forward.

"We're here to get all the dog paraphernalia for Misty."

"Misty?" AJ lifted his shoulders like he was totally in the dark about that name.

"Wilhelmina's dog?" Luke added. "Dani already found a great home for her and we promised we'd bring over Misty's dog bed, food bowl, food, and anything else that might be useful.

"Oh." All the steam rushed out of AJ's sails after Luke's explanation. I wanted to kiss him — Luke, not AJ — but that would have to wait. "But I heard you say you came looking for clues."

"Well, you never know what bit of something could be helpful. Alice told me that Wilhelmina called her last night. After I left," I added, hoping that would be a sufficient alibi.

"Alice who?" AJ finally pulled his little notebook out and jotted down something. He should have been doing that all along.

"Alice Cross—the person who agreed to adopt Misty. The person we have to bring all of the dog stuff to. Alice was sort of Wilhelmina's friend." I felt like I was talking to a four-year old.

"Sort of? What's that supposed to mean?"

"You'll have to ask Alice. I don't want to put words in her mouth."

I also had no intention of revealing the part about Wilhelmina meeting Brent. Especially since I wasn't positive that Alice remembered the conversation accurately or would remember to repeat it to AJ.

"At any rate, can we get the dog stuff now? For Alice?"

"You wait here. I'll bring it out." AJ disappeared into Wilhelmina's boat. I tapped my foot and wondered if there were any clues inside. Maybe Pip would discover something.

"That went well, don't you think?" Luke asked me.

"Yeah, peachy keen with a cherry on top. Next time I open my mouth around AJ, put your hand over it before something falls out that isn't supposed to."

Luke put his arm around my waist and gave it a squeeze. "It's one of your charming features, Dani. Besides, if I put my hand over your mouth, you'd probably bite it."

He was probably right. Bite before thinking or something like that.

13

AJ returned from inside Wilhelmina's boat with an armload of Misty's dog paraphernalia. I couldn't imagine how it had all fit in the boat leaving any room for Wilhelmina's belongings, let alone Wilhelmina herself. At least it showed that she put Misty's well-being front and center in her controversial world. And that made me especially happy knowing I'd found her a wonderful new home with Alice.

"Here you go, Dani. Oh, by the way. I called the committee about tonight's award ceremony and strongly suggested they postpone it. With Brent as one of the final four on the Best Business Award list, it seems the only solution for now. Brent was visibly relieved but the other two? Fit to be tied with all kinds of bad comments thrown my way." He shrugged. "Just a perk of my job. Rose promised to get the word out about the change."

I stifled a chuckle at Rose's ability to get her way without the other person even knowing it had been all her idea to begin with. "I'd say that's the right decision, AJ. Quick thinking on your part." He puffed up a little from my compliment. Nothing like a little ego stroking to get on his good side.

Luke took the pile of Misty's things from me. "Ready to go, Dani?"

"Yeah. Come on Pip. Oh," I stopped. "AJ? Is Maggie's surprise birthday party still a go for Sunday night or do we need to postpone that, too?" It wouldn't hurt to remind him that he'd asked me for a favor. It might get him to ease off a little on making me feel like one of the suspects for this murder.

"I'll stuff this in your car and be right back," Luke said, leaving me with AJ as he walked down the dock.

"What kind of question is that? I can't put the surprise off. Maggie's already giving me the cold shoulder ever since I told her I had to work. And that was *before* this murder. Now, maybe she'll understand my job sometimes has to come before her needs. But don't worry. I'll be at Sea Breeze one way or another, even if it's just a quick appearance to say *surprise*. Is it all set?"

"As far as I know. Lily and Sue Ellen have their heads together planning the food right now."

"Good. Thanks for helping, and thanks for finding a home for Misty. Now, I'd better get back inside."

Now what? Drop everything off at Alice's house and head to Sea Breeze? I hadn't made more than a couple of steps when Marcus jumped off his boat and caught up with me. "Did you think about my interview yet?"

"Actually, I did. If you have the other three on board for it, I'm in too." To help figure out if either of those three dropped any clues that might lead to who murdered Wilhelmina. They each had a motive as far as I was concerned.

"Really? You'll sit down with me and the other three business owners and talk about, oh, I don't know, maybe how to be creative with your businesses and how to bring in new customers?"

"Talk and listen. I think it will be very enlightening. Especially now that the award ceremony scheduled for tonight has been postponed by Detective Crenshaw." I was nearly to the end of the dock.

"What? When did that happen? Why? All my followers are waiting to find out who gets the Best Business Award in Misty Harbor. I promised that you'd share one of your Little Dog Diner recipes if you win."

Marcus had stopped walking. Apparently, this change didn't suit him, not that he had any say in it.

"What? Why did you promise that bit of nonsense?"

"It will bring you more exposure. I thought that's what I heard the winner would do." He looked like he was searching his fuzzy memory bank for something. "Anyway, Brent is planning to share *his* recipe for his famous chowder during the interview. Do you want to share anything like that?"

"No, and I can't imagine Brent would do that, either. Is this just one of your gimmicks to lure the readers of your blog to follow you and then make us look like we're going back on some nonexistent promise?"

I didn't believe anything this guy said, and I'd have to be extra careful during the interview that he didn't trick me into saying something I'd regret. Before I walked away from Marcus and his ridiculous comments, I asked, "Do you know if the marina manager is around?"

"Kyle? Great guy. It's hard to understand how he and Wilhelmina are related, though."

"What?"

"Yeah. I know. Crazy, huh? She's his aunt. Just goes to show how different people can be even when they're related. She wouldn't let Kyle enlarge the marina to make room for bigger boats, not that it's his final decision anyway. He'd have to run it by his father who's the owner, but Kyle does everything. My boat is the biggest allowed here."

Marcus looked back toward his boat and puffed his chest out a bit before he scanned the parking lot.

"I don't see Kyle's car here or over at his house." He pointed to a small, tidy cape-style house beyond the parking lot. "He's never gone for long, though. I'll see you here at two for the interview."

"Today? On your boat? Won't all of us be kind of squished?"

"Call it cozy."

"I have a better idea. Call the others and we'll meet at the Blueberry Bay Grapevine office. Since Rose is a sponsor for this weekend's events, you should be interviewing her, too. What do you think, Marcus?"

I didn't think he'd say no because I could see him salivating about having all of us do this interview. What was in it for him, I wondered? I had a niggling concern at the back of my head that I had to take control of this situation and not let Marcus lead us into some kind of trap.

"At four," I added.

"Okay." His reply was less than enthusiastic. "If you provide coffee and pie, I'll make it happen."

"Tomorrow," I added to give myself more time for strategizing. I stuck my hand out. "Deal?"

Marcus hesitated. Just like I suspected, there was something he wanted to get in his blog sooner rather than later.

"I'll check with the others and get back to you. They might be too busy with all the tourists flocking into town this weekend."

"No problem," I said feeling relieved that he didn't show much enthusiasm now that I'd set the parameters. "It was your idea. I'm sure you have plenty of other dirt to spread to all your followers."

Before I turned away, I didn't miss the angry look Marcus shot at me.

What the heck was he up to?

14

---

*L*uke had all of Misty's belongings stuffed behind the seat of the MG. If I didn't know better, I'd think we were heading to fill up a flea market booth.

"Where to now?" he asked.

"We need to deliver all this to Alice," I answered with an isn't-it-obvious expression added to my tone. I mean, the poor MG was stuffed to the roof.

"Just checking whether you had a stop on the way… like lunch maybe?"

"Alice first, then lunch," I said. "Can you wait that long?"

"I'll survive." An unmistakable stomach growl followed Luke's answer.

I ignored it because a small gray pickup pulled into the parking lot and stopped next to my MG.

"Perfect timing," I said to Luke, slamming my door closed before I'd had time to slide inside. I walked to the driver side of the truck. "Kyle Johnson?"

"That would be me. What can I do for you?" Kyle said as he unfolded his lanky body from his truck. "Danielle Mackenzie, right? I love your lobster rolls. And your blueberry pie. And your extra crispy grilled cheese." He let out a friendly laugh. "Okay, I won't lie. I love everything I've tried at the Little Dog Diner. And, probably everything I haven't sampled yet."

Kyle's friendly grin had me instantly liking him. Well, that and his obvious praise for my business didn't hurt.

"Great," Luke said. "Now, with all that food tempting me, I'm starving." He licked his lips. I felt a tiny bit bad for making him wait for lunch, but this was more important than filling our stomachs.

"Glad to hear it, Kyle, but it's pretty hard to mess up a lobster roll when the lobster meat is fresh from the ocean."

Pip sniffed Kyle's sneakers. "And, who do we have here?"

He reached down to let Pip sniff his hand before giving a friendly scratch behind her ears. "Cute bandana. I always enjoy seeing her outside the diner. "She's got quite the fan club," I said affectionately, smiling at his compliment as he straightened up and towered over me.

"So, you need to talk to me? Let me guess… it's about the infamous Wilhelmina Joy. That's all everyone is interested in at the moment."

Pip, not finding anything interesting around Kyle, moved off to the weeds and assorted trash at the edge of the lot. Wilhelmina did have a point about the trash problem.

"You're right. She's your aunt?" I asked, knowing the answer but it was a good way to bring up the connection.

"Guilty." Kyle smiled an easy-going grin that made me assume he was someone who enjoyed life to the fullest. "I know she annoyed a lot of people in Misty Harbor but deep down, she wasn't a bad person. Her shortcoming was her style."

He shrugged, giving me the impression there wasn't anything he could do about that trait of hers. "She didn't care what anyone thought about her, me included, and I'm probably her only relative that cared at all about her."

"She was lucky to have you in her life." And I meant it. Everyone, no matter how disagreeable they were, needed someone who loved them just the way they came. But who were the other relatives that Kyle referred to? Had Wilhelmina annoyed one of them to the point of turning them into a murderer?

"And Misty," he continued. "Wilhelmina doted on that dog but I'm really worried." Kyle looked around as if he expected Misty to come running over from somewhere. "I didn't know what happened to her. I just went to the animal shelter to check if she ended up there."

I touched Kyle's arm. "I'm so sorry. Someone should have told you that I offered to take Misty, or she would have ended up at the shelter. As a matter of fact," I pointed to all the items stuffed into my car, "Detective Crenshaw gave me all the dog items from your aunt's boat to deliver to her new owner."

"New owner?" A shadow passed over his face and my stomach lurched. What if *he* wanted Misty? I'd never considered a family member since I didn't know he was related to Wilhelmina until Marcus mentioned it. Alice would be devastated if Kyle took her away.

Luke, always so practical and levelheaded, said,

"I have an idea. Why don't you come with us to see Misty and the woman who hopes to adopt her?"

He glanced at me to see, I guessed, whether I was okay with his suggestion. It was brilliant.

"Great idea," I said. "Alice was friends with your aunt, and I'm sure she'd like to give you her condolences."

"Alice Cross? Aunt Willy would be happy for Misty to be living with her. Of all the people she ever mentioned, Alice was the only one who sparked the bit of kindness left in her. I hate to say this, but my aunt really wasn't a very happy person."

"Was Wilhelmina happy here on her boat? She's had it here for years, hasn't she?"

"I suppose she was happier here than anywhere else. Blueberry Bay was her passion... obsession actually. She couldn't stand to see any changes. Even here at the marina where my father wanted to upgrade the slips to accommodate bigger boats. She was a thorn in his side for sure, but now he can expand if he wants to. Nothing too big, but over the years, many of our regulars have mentioned they'd like to trade up. We've even lost some customers that already moved to bigger marinas."

Kyle shrugged. "Time will tell what happens. Nothing right away, I imagine."

That was an angle I hadn't considered — someone who wanted Wilhelmina out of the way so the marina could move up the boat ladder. At any rate, she angered someone enough to get herself killed and it had to be something connected to her obsession with protecting Blueberry Bay.

Luke's stomach growled again. When I looked at him, I couldn't ignore his pathetic, I'm starving expression. "Okay. How about we get lunch first." I turned to Kyle. "Would you like to join us? And then you can follow us over to see Alice and Misty."

"Sure. I never say no to an excuse to eat at the Little Dog Diner. Besides, there's nothing urgent here that can't wait until later this afternoon."

Luke fist bumped Kyle like they were in cahoots about this lunch arrangement. Maybe it was a guy thing. While we'd been chatting in the parking lot, AJ must have finished up his search of Wilhelmina's boat. He and his crew jumped off the back of her boat and walked down the dock toward us.

"I wonder if he found anything to help with the investigation," I mumbled to myself as I stepped in his path. "He's carrying several bags."

"Don't expect him to give you any information, Dani," Luke said. "Let's just go before you say something you'll regret."

"The only way to find out anything is to ask questions, Luke." I walked toward AJ. "Did you find anything, Detective?"

"As a matter of fact," he held up a crumpled Little Dog Diner bag. "I thought you told me that you didn't leave the muffins with Wilhelmina."

"I didn't. That bag you found could be from any time Wilhelmina bought something from the diner and brought it back to her boat, AJ. All that proves is that, even though she protested in front of the Little Dog Diner, she also chose to enjoy our delicious food." And, as I looked at the crumpled bag, a throw away item she despised so much, I found it interesting that she didn't practice what she preached.

I heard Luke cough, but suspected he was covering up a laugh at AJ's expense for my clever rebuttal of his silly insinuation. Really? A Little Dog Diner bag was the evidence he found?

If it *was* evidence, I hadn't left it there.

15

I sent Luke into the Little Dog Diner with Kyle to grab a booth and order lunch for me while I took a detour into the Blueberry Bay Grapevine office with Pip.

Rose, busy at her desk with her fingers flying over the keys of her old manual typewriter, didn't interrupt her concentration when we entered. She insisted the clickity clack chorus of the keys, mixed with the ding when she reached the right-hand margin was music to her ears.

My preference? Give me my computer any day where I could fix mistakes with a back arrow that I thought of as my magic wand.

"Rose?" I hated to interrupt but I needed to get

her up to speed on the new information I'd gathered at the marina.

She quickly held up one finger before continuing with her typing. I got a bowl of water for Pip while I waited, tapping my foot and hoping Rose was almost done instead of just beginning.

The click clack of the keys stopped. "*Fini!*" She pulled the paper out with a flourish. "Now, to get this added to the front page of the Blueberry Bay Grapevine, printed, distributed, and… on the Grapevine's face book page, too. I hope Marcus doesn't bust a gut when I beat him with this head-liner praising Wilhelmina." She laughed and leaned back in her chair with a contented sigh. "Actually, I couldn't care less what he busts when he sees this. What do you think?"

I took the paper and read the headline out loud. "*Wilhelmina Joy: A Force of Nature Keeping Blueberry Bay Pristine.*"

"I love it, Rose. This way you get to set the tone for a celebration of life and what was good about Wilhelmina instead of what Marcus's intention probably is—to trash her and stir up trouble."

"That's my plan, dear. I never did like that man." She set the article on her desk and turned her attention to me. "What's new with you?"

I could barely contain my excitement. "You won't believe it, Rose. Wilhelmina had a whole different mission that we didn't know anything about." After I sat down, Pip jumped into my lap and followed the conversation intently while I scratched the sensitive spot on her chest.

"Really?"

"Really. I had a chat with Kyle at the marina. Super nice guy, by the way. Anyway, he let it out that his father wants to expand the Misty Marina so bigger boats can moor there."

"And? I think I see where this might be going." Rose crossed her arms and waited for me to continue.

"Apparently, Wilhelmina had some kind of power over the decision, and she had managed to prevent any expansion while she was alive."

Rose slipped her reading glasses off and dangled them between two fingers. "Bigger boats? That's exactly what Larry has been grumbling about for quite some time for his tour business. I never knew the reason behind halting the expansion stopped with Wilhelmina, though."

"I know, right? It sure gives Larry a huge motive to get that roadblock, in the name of Wilhelmina Joy, out of the way." I eased Pip off my lap and stood up. "AJ was searching her boat when Luke and I went to get Misty's stuff. He found a crumpled up Little Dog Diner bag and implied that it proved I'd lied to him about leaving muffins when I went to visit her last night."

"That's weak at best. I know she railed against sugary content, but that woman had a sweet tooth and tried to hide it." Rose leaned back in her chair. "I wonder what else she was hiding that would hurt her image as the self-appointed savior of Blueberry Bay."

Pip had wandered to her dog bed and curled up, apparently resigned to the idea that nothing exciting was about to happen.

"Luke and Kyle are waiting for me at the diner. Plus, I need to see how Christy and Chad are handling their first day without me looking over their shoulders."

Rose harrumphed. "Those two will surprise you, Danielle. Give them space and you'll be able to take more time off. The worst thing is for the boss to watch every single move."

I suspected Rose was right because that's exactly how I felt when she was training Lily and me to take over the diner. But still, I felt a stab of remorse that they *didn't* need me there. I wanted it both ways.

Rose laughed. I knew she saw right through my pursed lips and wrinkled brow. "You and I are still the owners, Danielle, but having a bit of freedom from the diner is exactly what you need. Especially once Luke starts the renovations at Sea Breeze to add the new apartment for me. He'll need lots of help."

That hadn't been settled yet as far as I was concerned, but I didn't want to have that argument now.

"Why not?" Rose asked with a twitch at the edge of her lips.

"Why not what?" I had a sinking feeling that what I thought I was saying to myself, had actually fallen out of my mouth. Again. I slapped the side of my head wondering if I'd ever learn to control that bad habit of mine.

"You know as well as I do that Luke will be much more comfortable moving into Sea Breeze after you two are married if I have a separate apartment. You don't need me hovering over the two of you day and night. He and I have agreed on the plan, and the sooner you jump on board with this project, the quicker we'll get it done."

Rose grabbed her big hobo bag and slipped it

over her shoulder. "I'm feeling hungry. Okay if I join you at the diner?"

The lack of any room for an argument let me know I'd lost this one in a big way. But it didn't distract me from reading through her motivation of joining me for lunch. "Of course, and I'm sure Kyle will love to chat with you about that marina expansion."

I hooked my arm around her waist and we both laughed. Sometimes it felt like we communicated more by what we *didn't* say.

Leaving Pip curled in her dog bed, we walked to the diner, ready to tackle anything.

Together, we were formidable. Or, so I liked to tell myself.

My heart fluttered when Luke stood up and waved at us when we walked into the diner. Kyle, sitting with his back to us, turned and smiled. Just when I thought I was going to have a pleasant lunch and learn more about the Misty Marina, Larry stepped in front of me with a nasty sneer on his face.

I pulled up short, ready to flee, as if he were a hunter and I was the prey.

"Just who I was looking for," he said. "And, my lucky day with both the esteemed Rose Mackenzie and her meddling granddaughter in the same place at the same time."

Meddling? What was he talking about?

"I'll tell you exactly what I'm talking about." He answered a comment I thought I'd kept to myself. But, once again, my thoughts must have fallen out of my mouth. He jabbed his finger at Rose's chest.

"You got the award ceremony postponed. You should be ashamed of yourself with all your interfering tactics."

Rose stepped right up to Larry, drew herself to her full five-foot-seven-inch frame, and said, "Detective Crenshaw made the call to give everyone a breather. What's your rush, Larry? Don't forget that the committee judges on personality, patience, and presentation when they pick their winner. You might want to adjust your attitude, or you'll never have a chance."

Larry's mouth dropped open.

Before he could compose himself and shoot a nasty refrain back at Rose, I jumped into the conversation with the question that I wanted answered. "Where were you last night when Wilhelmina went to the Savory Soup & Sandwich Café, Larry?"

"Home getting rested for the weekend, not that it's any business of yours, Danielle."

"It's interesting that Wilhelmina Joy was the reason the Misty Marina couldn't expand. I heard from a reliable source that the marina will expand now that she's gone. With her out of the way, you'll get what you want—a bigger boat to upgrade your Blueberry Bay and Beyond Tour Company."

His finger jabbed at me now. "You listen to me." Larry's words hissed out like a venomous snake. "Watch what you imply before someone shuts *you* up, too." He strode past us to the door.

"Was that a threat?" I asked Rose.

"Yes," Larry answered before he walked out and slammed the door.

16

*L*uke dashed to my side while I remained frozen in place. As Larry's words repeated in my head, I turned into a trembling mess.

"What happened?" he asked me tenderly while he held me around my waist and guided me to the booth.

"I've never been a fan of Larry's," Rose said with a dismissive shake of her hand. "I don't know *who* on the award committee thought he was worthy of consideration of the award. In my opinion, he doesn't have one shred of the qualities needed to get the title of Best Business in Misty Harbor."

"What did he say?" Luke asked again after we were settled.

"Something like watch what you say before

someone shuts you up," Rose said. "Danielle, honey, I wouldn't worry about that piece of fish bait."

"I'm not so sure," Kyle piped in. "There were more times than I can recall when I heard him give Aunt Wilhelmina a tongue lashing about her protesting against the marina expansion. He can be brutal with his words."

"Great," I muttered. "Just what I need, a raving lunatic out to get *me*, now." I looked at the others in the booth. "What if *he* is the murderer? If he killed Wilhelmina to get her out of his way so the expansion could proceed, what would stop him from doing the same thing to me to get me out of the way of the Best Business Award? He's acting kind of crazy."

"We'd better tell AJ about this threat. That will put Larry on notice at least," Luke said. "If he knows the police are watching his moves, he'll have to—"

"What?" I asked. "Be extra careful while he stalks me?"

My fear had morphed into anger now. "I refuse to let him intimidate me. I plan to stand up to that kind of bullying, that's for sure."

Luke squeezed my hand. It helped having him on my side.

Christy arrived at our booth with a tray over-loaded with our order. I guess Luke wasn't kidding when he said he was hungry.

"How's it going here?" I asked her as she set the fried haddock sandwich and fries platter in front of Luke. Kyle got a big bowl of clam chowder with warm rolls on the side, and my plate had my favorite tuna melt with cheddar cheese and tomato.

Yum, I said to myself as I stared at the food in front of me. The delicious aroma plus all the tension had fired up my appetite in a big way.

"I wasn't sure what you wanted for lunch, Dani. I hope that's okay." Luke eyed my tuna melt like he wouldn't mind if I said I didn't want it so he could have it for dessert. I reached for one of the crispy fries on his plate.

"Help yourself to my fries," he added since he didn't really have a choice.

Christy laughed as we stuffed the food into our mouths. "Everything here is going as smooth as chocolate mousse pie, so if you're still busy, Chad and I have the diner covered and under control."

Rose winked at me when I glanced at her. She had to rub it in that she was right. Again.

"What can I get for *you*, Rose?" Christy asked, her pad poised for an order.

"Oh, how about the salmon salad and a water with lemon," she said without glancing at the menu. After all this time, she knew it inside and out. She set her floppy straw hat on the seat next to Kyle.

"I'll be right back with that." Christy tucked the pad in her apron pocket and walked to the kitchen. I heard her yell the order to Chad as she picked up the next loaded tray for another booth. I relaxed and said a silent thank you that these two people were competent and loving their jobs.

Once Christy was out of hearing range, Rose turned toward Kyle. "So, tell me more about Larry and Wilhelmina and the marina expansion."

Nothing like getting right to the point.

"I don't want to spread any rumors or get anyone in trouble."

"Too late for that, dear," Rose said. "There's been a murder and now everything is fair game. Especially since Larry just threatened Dani. Now, it's not a rumor if you witnessed these arguments between Larry and your aunt."

"Like I told Dani already, a lot of people in town weren't crazy about Aunt Willy."

"Hated her more like it, from how you've described their interactions. Maybe even enough to kill her?" Rose said, not one to mince words.

Kyle squirmed in the booth but there was zero chance of him getting away from this interrogation since Rose had him blocked in.

"I'm trying to be diplomatic. Aunt Willy had her abrasive side, but she was still my aunt, and I did my best to look out for her. And Larry had strong words with her for sure, but he was always professional in his dealings with me."

"Fair enough, Kyle." Rose patted his arm. He looked like a few tears might overflow the rim of his eyes, but he pulled himself together.

I felt sorry for him. Here, he'd lost his aunt, and we were all bashing her, while he seemed to have cared for in his way. He needed time to mourn.

"Larry came to the marina a lot since he has his tour boat moored there. That's probably why the two of them got into so many screaming matches." Kyle took a few spoonsful of chowder as if the food might give him energy for this difficult conversation.

I took a bite of my tuna melt, realizing that Chad had done a superb job of broiling it to perfection. It had a bit of crispness on the edges and the cheese was melted but not runny. His sandwich was better than mine if I was honest about it.

Kyle continued, "They had their worst arguments when Larry had tourists boarding for a trip.

Aunt Willy would hand them fliers, telling them about all the trash he'd dump into Blueberry Bay. That part wasn't even true, and I told her that Larry was very careful with any disposable items, leaving nothing in the ocean. She said it gave her protest more umph and kept harassing his customers anyway. Larry even changed his tactic recently and tried to reason with Aunt Willy, telling her that the ocean was his livelihood, and he planned to protect it. She dismissed him with a flick of her wrist and said the marina would never expand to accommodate the bigger boat he wanted."

Wow. Wilhelmina was more devious than I'd imagined, stooping to lies to hurt her target. I had to wonder what else she'd had up her sleeve for Brent's café and my diner.

I put my sandwich down and looked at Kyle directly. "Do you have any idea if she had plans to meet anyone on Thursday night or why she went to Brent's Savory Soup & Sandwich Café?" Besides Alice, he seemed to be the only other person she might have confided in.

"I was just doing my nightly walk-around for a last boat check at nine that night when I saw Aunt Willy and Misty leaving her boat. They headed off the dock. It was an odd time for her to be going out so I waited to ask if I could help her with anything."

I held my breath.

"She had her sign with her, which was odd, but I was used to her unusual behavior."

I watched Kyle's expression change to a deep sadness.

"If I had stopped her like my gut instinct told me to do, maybe this terrible tragedy would have been averted."

"Maybe, but hindsight is always twenty-twenty, Kyle," I said as soothingly as possible. "Did she tell you where she was going?"

"Yes. She said she had some business at the Savory Soup & Sandwich Café."

His head dropped onto the palm of his hand. Rose put her arm around his shoulder in a comforting gesture. "Don't blame yourself. Wilhelmina put herself in danger."

That was true, and we needed to bring the murderer to justice.

There were too many possibilities and it saddened me to think that Brent might be at the top of the list.

Who met her at the café?

And why?

17

I excused myself from the booth, leaving Luke, Rose, and Kyle to continue their conversation without me. Christy intercepted my route to the kitchen to talk to Chad.

"About the bill?" she asked, obviously nervous to ask me, her boss, about this awkward situation.

"Great question. Everyone's lunch is my treat. Oh, and Christy? Could you bring over a bag with six oatmeal chocolate chip cookies to go?"

"Sure thing, Dani."

I slipped her my credit card and entered the kitchen where sizzles and aromas assaulted my senses like a well-worn comfy sweater.

"Chad?" I said. "Great cooking." Relief crossed

his face, erasing the worry lines I'd seen when he saw me enter.

"Thank you, Dani. That means a lot. I'm really getting the hang of the pace and all the tips you showed me are second nature now. Of course, having Christy here, too, is great since we work so seamlessly together."

I patted his back. "Thanks so much. Being able to have some down time is great for me."

He put his spatula down and wiped his hands on his grease-spattered apron. "Anything new about the murder? Christy is hearing all kinds of chitchat from the customers, but you know how a story grows and changes with each telling. Someone even said that Wilhelmina was killed because she dumped all her trash on Hidden Treasures doorstep. I'd imagine that John Harmon would be mighty angry if that's true."

"I haven't heard about that, but do you know anything about the Misty Marina expanding?"

"Not about an expansion, but someone else heard that Wilhelmina was killed because someone wanted her boat slip. Being at the end like she was, she had a coveted spot apparently."

Chad lifted the basket filled with haddock from the deep fryer and left it to drain. I was impressed how well he moved between the deep fryer, the griddle, and mixing up salads all while discussing Wilhelmina's murder with me.

I was lucky with this hard-working pair; both were definitely keepers.

"All set for the day?" I asked, not wanting to make any assumptions if he felt he needed more than Christy's help.

"You bet. I've never enjoyed a job so much. As a matter of fact, it doesn't even feel like work." A grin spread across his face, which let me know Rose and I had made the absolute right choice when we hired Chad and Christy.

Now what? I asked myself. Since they had the diner under control, I could do a bit of investigating to get this murder behind Misty Harbor... and me, just in case Larry's threat meant something more than angry talk. I had to take his words about someone shutting me up seriously.

First up, though, was taking Kyle to visit Alice and Misty.

I slid in next to Luke, glad to see that Christy had cleared everyone's plates away. She set big pieces of blueberry pie with vanilla ice cream in front of both Luke and Kyle and a bag with my oatmeal chocolate chip cookies in front of me.

"Want a bite?" Luke asked me with his fork dripping melting ice cream, poised in my direction.

I hated to deprive him of his own blueberries, but I said, "Of course," and opened my mouth for the delicious treat.

"Just one bite though," he said after my mouth was filled, and I couldn't complain.

The two pieces of pie disappeared in almost a blink of an eye.

"Ready to visit Alice and Misty now?" I asked Kyle.

"Yes, then, unfortunately I'll have to get back to work. I have to move Aunt Willy's boat since someone else has been champing at the bit for that spot."

"Really?" Chad's comment of a few minutes earlier wasn't a rumor after all. "Who, if you don't mind me asking?"

Kyle leaned over the table and whispered. "Brent and Josie. They have a boat waiting for a slip to open up here. I was wondering if that's why Aunt Willy was at Brent's café last night. I'm just speculating, but maybe he wanted to talk to her about moving her boat since she hasn't taken it out on the ocean all year. She only lives there and could put it somewhere else."

I stared at Kyle. My eyes fluttered open and closed many times before I could respond. "That's kind of a bombshell bit of information."

"Let's not jump to any conclusions," Rose said wisely.

Was it Kyle's intention to get a rumor started to deflect attention away from himself? Kyle and his father had a lot to gain with Wilhelmina out of the way, so to speak. With a marina expansion, there would be higher slip fees bringing in a lot more money. After all, he knew Wilhelmina better than anyone. Did *he* have something to hide by pointing to someone else who didn't like his Aunt Willy?

My list of the possible suspects just got longer — Brent and Josie to save the café and get a coveted slip at the marina, Larry to get a bigger boat for his tour company if the marina expanded, John to end the protesting, and now Kyle and his father.

Holy lobsterolly, this was getting confusing.

Rose slid out of the booth, allowing Kyle to extricate himself, too. I doubted that he'd expected this kind of interrogation when he accepted my invitation for lunch.

"I'll get Pip, and you can get back to your paper, Rose, while we take Kyle over to visit with Alice and Misty."

"Kyle," I said, "you'll be so impressed with how well those two have already bonded." I didn't plan to give him much wiggle room to take Misty away from Alice.

"Thanks for lunch," Kyle said. "I don't know what Aunt Willy was thinking by protesting in front of the best eating place in Misty Harbor. It's not like she didn't enjoy a muffin or a bowl of chowder every now and again herself. I sure hope Detective Crenshaw finds her killer soon."

Me too, I said to myself. Me too.

When I walked toward the Blueberry Bay Grapevine's office, I was surprised to see Marcus heading for the same destination. From his determined stride and clenched fists, I assumed he wasn't stopping by for a pleasant chat with Rose.

"You think you can get away with bullying everyone to do your bidding?" he yelled at Rose. "There's no need to postpone the award ceremony."

"Calm down, Marcus," Rose said. Like she was talking to a four-year old that couldn't find his favorite blankie. "AJ made the decision. If you want to take it up with him, go ahead. What's the big deal?"

"My blog followers are expecting to find out who the winner is *tonight*, not tomorrow night. I planned a big give away to get them to tune in. They don't take kindly when the plan changes and it makes me look like a liar just to get their attention."

"I suppose Wilhelmina didn't like the plan change to her life, either. Have you forgotten what happened to her? It seems all you can think about is how *you've* been inconvenienced?" Rose yelled back.

Kyle walked over to Marcus and put his arm around the older man's shoulder. "I know you weren't a fan of Aunt Willy's, but have a little respect, man. She never did anything to you except give you material for your blog."

Marcus raised his eyebrows.

"Yeah, I follow it, and I think you're making a mountain out of this tragedy for your own benefit. Your followers don't care half as much as you think they do about who wins the Best Business Award. I think you just want the award presentation to happen so you can spin it to imply that the winner might have killed Aunt Willy before the bad publicity hurt them too much."

"Really, Marcus?" I was stunned at Kyle's accusation. "Is that what this is all about? Your stupid blog?"

"I'll have you know that my blog has more followers than The Blueberry Bay Grapevine. The future is online, not on paper." He directed his comment at Rose who didn't wilt under his glare. Actually, she smiled.

"Forget the interview," I said to Marcus. "I've changed my mind and I'll be talking to the others and suggest they have nothing to do with you. You don't have our interests at heart."

Marcus pointed at me. "You'll regret this, Dani." He stomped back to his car and sped away.

"Wow. You really know how to get under peoples' skin today," Luke said. "I think both Larry and Marcus will be unfriending you on Facebook."

With friends like them, who needed enemies? This weekend hadn't officially started, and I couldn't wait for it to end?

But where would it lead in the meantime?

18

*A*lice, with Misty at her side, grinned from ear to ear when she opened her door for me.

Until she saw Kyle standing behind me.

"Come in," she said, keeping her focus on Kyle. It was obvious she was worried about something, probably that he'd come to take Misty.

Pip darted inside and gave Misty a quick sniff in greeting. We all followed.

"Misty looks so relaxed and happy," I said, hoping to break the tension that had fallen over our visit. "Do you know Wilhelmina's nephew, Kyle?"

"I do," Alice replied, still looking wary.

"He's so happy that you have Misty, but when he heard that we were bringing over all of the dog supplies from Wilhelmina's boat, he asked if he could come and visit her, too."

"Where do you want Misty's things?" Luke asked, balancing the pile of food and bowls on top of the dog bed.

"Oh, the food could go in the kitchen if you don't mind, but I'd like her bed in the living room next to my chair."

"No problem," Luke said, following Alice to the living room.

I was a little worried that Kyle hadn't said anything yet, but I also noticed that Misty stayed close to Alice and barely even gave him a second glance. That made me think they didn't have much of a relationship.

With Misty's bed in place next to her chair, Alice directed Luke to take the food to the kitchen. "Through that door. If you leave everything on the counter, I'll put it away after you all leave."

"Okay, Alice," he said, and left us alone.

I handed Alice the bag from the Little Dog Diner.

"You shouldn't have," she said, but I could tell she was only being polite. She certainly wasted no time peeking inside the bag. "Oh my, cookies. I'll save these for later when I have my afternoon tea."

With that, she sat in her chair and rested her hand on Misty's head. "Make yourselves comfortable," she offered when Luke returned from the kitchen.

"Are you sure Misty isn't any trouble for you?" Kyle asked after he sat down.

"Oh, not at all. She's already figured out the dog door and lets herself out into the back yard. Mostly, though, she sits right here next to me." Alice stroked Misty's soft fur as if to demonstrate their bond. "I couldn't ask for a better companion. You aren't planning to take her back, are you? I think Wilhelmina would be happy with her right here with me." The stern, teacherly tone cut through any pretense of Kyle's possible intentions.

Kyle looked at me, then rubbed his chin.

I held my breath.

Alice sat at the edge of her chair.

Misty's eyes stayed on Alice.

What on earth was he waiting for? "Kyle?" I asked.

"To be honest, I was planning to take her with me back to the marina where I'd assumed, she'd be the most comfortable. You know, a familiar place and all. I was afraid she'd be too much for you, Alice, but I can see that Misty has found the perfect place right here."

Kyle smiled as he looked at Alice and Misty, but it had a sad quality at the same time.

I could breathe again.

Alice let out a sigh from deep in her chest. "Thank you, my dear boy. You've just made an old lady happier than you can imagine."

"But, could I come visit once in a while?" he asked, almost as if he expected Alice to say no.

"Of course, you can. Come anytime. We'd both love your company, right Misty?"

We all looked at the dog. She wagged her tail enthusiastically at the sound of her name.

Kyle relaxed back into the chair and looked around the cozy room. "Is that Blueberry Bay?" he asked as his gaze stopped on the beautiful quilt hanging on Alice's wall.

"Yes. My pride and joy. It's funny, but I never noticed that along with the rest of Misty Harbor, your marina is right there at the edge of the bay, but now I'll think of Wilhelmina every time I look at this quilt."

This visit went better than I ever expected. "Perfect," I said, basking under the glow of Alice's beautiful quilt. "Before Luke and I leave, I'm wondering if you remembered anything more about your conversation with Wilhelmina last night."

"I'm glad you asked, or I would have forgotten to tell you this. Seeing the marina on the quilt made me remember something she told me. She said Kyle's father threatened to move her boat to make room for someone who actually planned to use the slip for more than just living on their boat. Can you believe it? What difference would it make if she never left the marina? She paid for the spot, didn't she?"

"Actually, she was behind in her payments," Kyle said softly. "Aunt Willy hadn't paid anything this whole year. She said she didn't have the money, and my father wouldn't have the nerve to evict an old woman."

"Oh my!" Alice's hand covered her mouth. "Your father wouldn't treat a relative like that, would he?"

"I'm afraid the decision was final. Besides, my dad is only related by marriage, and he never liked Aunt Willy. Not paying for her prime slip was all the excuse he needed to move her out of the spotlight at the marina. Now, there won't be any vocal resistance from her, which I'm sure, makes my dad happier than a clam at high tide."

We all stared at Kyle like he'd just pulled the pin

out of a grenade. We held our breath waiting for it to explode.

"What?" he asked.

"Kyle, you just gave your father a motive for killing Wilhelmina," I said, not believing that he hadn't thought of this already. "Where was he last night?"

Shock slowly filled Kyle's face as this new perspective became clear. His eyes bugged open wide and he clenched his bottom lip between his teeth. "My father? He was home as far as I know." He shook his head quickly. "But it doesn't matter, he *wouldn't* kill Aunt Willy. He *didn't* kill her."

"Which is it, Kyle?" I asked. "He wouldn't or he didn't? There is a difference. And, for the record, I'm not accusing him of killing her. I'm only suggesting that he might be on Detective Crenshaw's radar when this boat moving business comes to light."

Kyle's mouth opened.

I raised my finger before he could protest any more. "It will come to light. You can be sure of that."

"Oh dear." Alice rubbed her hands together and pressed them to her heart. "What did I start? All I want is to give poor Misty all the love and attention she deserves."

"It's okay, Alice. Of course, you haven't started anything. The facts always find their way to the surface, and the facts are what will help solve this terrible murder. Isn't that what we all want?"

"Of course," Kyle said, almost too quickly.

"It must almost be time for your tea and a cookie, Alice. And, it's time for us to get a move on." I stood up and waited for Kyle to make a move.

"I'll be by for a visit with you and Misty," he said before he walked to the door.

Luke and Pip followed me, and we all left.

"Kyle?" I asked. "Did Brent or Josie harass Wilhelmina about her boat slip?"

"Brent came to the marina a couple of times. He wasn't like Larry when he talked to Aunt Willy, but I could tell he was frustrated about waiting. Why?"

"There seems to be a small circle of people with strong motives and big gains with Wilhelmina dead."

"Well, my father didn't kill her. If you want my opinion, I'd put my money on Larry. He bullied Aunt Willy every chance he had to back off on blocking the marina expansion. When that didn't work, he killed her."

"You might be right," I said, remembering how Larry had threatened me only a few hours earlier. He was someone who wanted everything his way, and he'd made it perfectly clear that he didn't want me talking about any of this.

Was he desperate enough for this bigger boat to kill someone?

19

I waited for Kyle to leave before I pulled the MG out of Alice's driveway. Pip positioned herself in her usual spot—paws on the dashboard and her back legs rooted on Luke's lap, ready for anything.

"Where to now?" he asked.

"I'm supposed to help Lily and Sue Ellen plan Maggie's surprise birthday party. They expected me at Sea Breeze hours ago."

"But?" He looked at me with a grin, which told me he knew that wouldn't be our next stop.

I headed out into the street and pulled my visor down to shield my eyes from a sudden burst of blinding sun. "But... I need to talk to the three other

Best Business Award finalists about Marcus's interview. I told him to forget about my participation. That went over about as well as if he'd discovered a hole in the hull of his precious boat. Now, I want to be sure the others aren't going to go behind my back."

"You can't really control what they do, Dani." Luke kept one hand on Pip and used the other to shade his eyes from the harsh rays. "They might think the publicity will be good for their businesses."

"True, but I plan to convince them that Marcus will most likely make them look like fools at best, or murderers, at worst. His game is all about providing sensation for his blog readers. What will *they* gain as business owners by doing the interview? I suspect that Marcus will manage to make it all about himself at their expense. At least, that's my take-away about his strategy and the least I can do is share that with the others." I braked suddenly as an out-of-state car suddenly stopped in front of me to take in the view, I supposed, of Blueberry Bay.

I could feel Luke's eyes burning into me. "You don't like Marcus, do you?"

I glanced at Luke while I considered his question. "When I first met him after Wilhelmina kicked me off her boat, he made me laugh and seemed neighborly. The more I hear about him, though, I think he's got an agenda. He's not about putting a good light on Misty Harbor or our businesses. Mine included. He goaded Wilhelmina every chance he got just to have fodder for his blog. My gut instinct tells me that his interview will be more of the same, and I'm not going to play his game."

With that, I stopped in front of the Savory Soup & Sandwich Café.

Luke held my arm, holding me hostage in the MG. I didn't mind. He could have said keep driving for all I cared. I could think of more interesting ways to spend a few hours with Luke.

With his eyes all serious, he asked, "Do you believe Kyle's theory about Larry murdering Wilhelmina because he bullied her?"

Darn. He didn't have plans for us to whisk away for a quiet afternoon somewhere. Not that leaving town would solve any problems, but it would be a welcomed change.

"He's got a valid point," I said, resigning myself to continue plodding along for answers. "But I have to wonder if Kyle is desperate to take the focus off his father or even himself. I mean, Misty Marina has a lot to gain if they have a clear path to expansion now. But I do think Kyle had a soft spot for his aunt, and I don't think he killed her. It didn't sound like his father shared that fondness, though. Sometimes, money motivates people to do the unthinkable, especially if they have an unexpected opportunity."

"Like following Wilhelmina and making it look like Brent killed her in his café?"

"Exactly."

Luke brushed a few stray curls from my eyes, reminding me, as if I could ever forget, why I agreed to marry him. But the romantic bubble burst when he said, "So, you don't think Brent killed her?"

I sighed away my romantic thoughts and rested my head against his shoulder. "In the long run, it doesn't matter what I think, Luke. I want to get to the bottom of this before someone tries to shut me up like they silenced Wilhelmina."

"That's what Larry threatened, and it makes me worry." As if to show his concern, Luke gently stroked my cheek. Pip must have sensed our concern because she stuck her face in mine and gave me a lick.

I jerked my head away from her tongue and wiped the slobber off my cheek. "Ewww. Not helpful, Pipster." But it did make me laugh which helped ease the tension of my situation.

"I know you're worried, Luke. I am too, which puts me on a short clock because, like I already said, I'm not letting anyone bully me into shutting up." With that, I pulled away from his comforting embrace and slid out of the MG.

Pip didn't wait for Luke to get out. She jumped over my seat and darted to the café before I could attach her leash. At least she'd get AJ's attention so I could ask him some questions.

Sure enough, AJ, scowl in place, emerged from the café with Pip in his arms. If I didn't know better, I'd think this was Pip's plan all along—her way to speed up this murder investigation.

"Dani! How many times do I have to tell you to keep Pip out of my investigation?"

"Sorry, AJ. Maybe you need to tell her instead of me since she kind of has a mind of her own." I tried to make light of the situation but from the deepening frown on his face, I failed.

He deposited Pip in my arms. From the way she gave my chin a happy lick when AJ turned back toward the café, Pip knew where she belonged.

"You've made a few people upset by changing the award ceremony, AJ," I said, hoping he'd hear me out. "They're blaming Rose for pushing her weight around. And me, too. Larry and Marcus both gave me veiled threats." I called all this to AJ's retreating back. He stopped.

Apparently, I got his attention.

"They threatened you?" He walked back toward me, standing with Luke and Pip.

"Larry told me that if I didn't stop talking about Wilhelmina's murder, someone might shut me up, too."

"Shut you up, as in, murder you?"

I had my hands full with Pip bouncing in my arms, but I said, "Honestly, AJ, you're the detective. I can't read his mind, but he was angry and those were his parting words as he left the diner after lunch." I had his undivided attention now. "Have you heard about how Larry bullied Wilhelmina?"

AJ crossed his arms. "I'm listening."

"We were just talking to Kyle, the marina manager, and he said that Larry and Wilhelmina had many arguments. And…" I paused for effect. "She harassed his customers when they were preparing to leave on one of his boat tours. She'd tell them that Larry dumped his trash into the bay."

"Maybe he did."

"Kyle said it was a lie and Larry even tried to reason with his aunt. She didn't care if it wasn't true. She used it an effective accusation to get her point across."

I waited for all that to sink in. "And—"

"There's more?" AJ sounded frustrated. I'm sure he had to wonder how I'd learned so much while he was still stuck here going over the crime scene.

"Maybe you already know this, but Larry's been itching for a bigger tour boat. Wilhelmina, meanwhile, managed to block any expansion at Misty Marina."

I shrugged and turned both my hands toward the sky. "Now, with Wilhelmina gone, the expansion can go forward and Larry can get his bigger boat."

"Okay." AJ pulled his notebook out. "One, Larry and Wilhelmina had a history of arguing. Two, Larry threatened you. And, three, Wilhelmina was the reason Misty Marina couldn't expand, preventing Larry from getting a bigger tour boat."

He quirked his eyebrow at me. "Is there more?"

"Not that I'm aware of. Yet. So, what have *you* got, AJ?"

"Nice try. You know I can't share anything with

you." He lowered his voice. "I do have one thing you can help me with, though."

I waited.

AJ looked at Luke. "Do you mind giving me a minute alone with Dani?"

I nodded to Luke.

He took Pip and ambled down the walk.

With his voice barely above a whisper, AJ said, "No one knows how Wilhelmina was murdered except you, since you found the body. Have you told anyone?"

I shook my head, even though I had told Luke. However, I didn't think AJ needed to know that right now.

"Good. Let's keep it that way. It's unusual and if someone slips up, they'll reveal themselves as the murderer."

"I can do that."

"And, Dani? Be careful. Don't take Larry's threat lightly."

I appreciated Luke's softer tone. "I guess I should tell you that Marcus sort of threatened me, too."

"Jeez. What the heck have you been up to for the past," he looked at his watch, "six or seven hours? Before I know it, you'll have every person who ever looked at Wilhelmina yesterday mad at you and then, I'll get a 9-1-1 call that you're in some kind of danger."

"Don't be so dramatic," I answered.

I *was* worried, but I didn't want AJ to know, or he might lock me up for my own safety.

*a*s I watched AJ duck under the yellow crime scene tape and disappear inside the café, a light tap on my shoulder made me jump a foot off the ground. And yelp, too.

I swung around, ready for anything, only to find Maggie laughing at me. "A little jittery, Dani?"

"You surprised me, that's all." Of course, I was edgy after the morning I'd had with both Larry and Marcus trying to intimidate me. "I was thinking about something else."

When Maggie crouched down, Pip ran over for her dose of love, leaping into her arms, and almost knocking her over backwards. It would have served her right for scaring me.

"Hello, Miss Pipsqueak. I'm glad to see you,

too," Maggie cooed while Pip lavished her special brand of doggie kisses on Maggie's face.

Pip wiggled and yapped her greeting before Luke handed her leash to me.

"Okay." Maggie stood up and dusted off Pip's hair from her jeans. "Spill it, Dani," she said. "What have you got? I know you, and I know you've uncovered something." She looped her arm through mine and steered me away from the café… and AJ.

"What did you discover so far while you've been working for Brent and Josie?" I asked, hoping she had something.

"I told them I couldn't help unless they were totally honest with me."

"And they confessed to the murder?" I suspected that was wishful thinking but, you never know.

"Not at all, but Brent is in deep swirling water." She looked around, pulled me close on one side and Luke on the other. "He admitted that he met Wilhelmina at his café last night around nine."

My hand flew to cover my mouth. "No." I said in disbelief. This added an important detail to the news from Kyle, that Wilhelmina had business at the café at nine.

"*Why* did he meet her?" I asked Maggie.

We walked farther away from the café before

Maggie continued. "I had to pull it out of Brent, but he told me that he offered Wilhelmina money to stop the protest. He's scared to death that AJ will find out, accuse him of murder, and throw him in jail."

"Well, yeah, the cards are certainly stacked against him. And, he wanted Wilhelmina's slip at the marina."

"What?" Maggie's huge eyes popped wide open. "How can they afford a boat? They're paying me with free soup and sandwiches for the rest of my life. Something isn't right with this picture."

"I agree."

"Don't you two go jumping to conclusions about Brent and Josie's money situation," Luke said, jumping into our conversation with his usual common sense observations. "Maybe there's a simple explanation. All I know is that they're both hard workers and speaking as a businessman myself, I suspect the profit margin at Savory Soups & Sandwiches is slim."

"Good point," I said. "Josie took the job as dispatcher instead of working full time for Brent. That tells me they needed a regular paycheck instead of relying on the ups and downs of the café."

Maggie held her hands up in surrender. "Okay. I get your point. But still, maybe they should think about selling their boat to get some money instead of having it drain away their limited funds."

I held my finger to my lips as I looked over Maggie's shoulder. "Shhh. Here comes Brent."

"Yeah, we planned to meet here."

"Hey, Brent." I waved him over. "I was hoping to run into you."

"Why?" The suspicious tone in his voice set me back, as well as his hangdog look. Normally, he'd been friendly and happy to see me. I suppose I shouldn't be surprised. He had so many problems hitting him from every direction, he probably expected a new disaster every time he turned around.

"Well, Marcus approached me about doing an interview with the four Best Business finalists—you, me, Larry, and John. I wanted to talk to you about it."

Brent stood in front of me with his thumbs hooked in his pants pockets.

"I can't stand that guy. I'm not interested." His stance screamed back off.

"Interesting, Brent, because he told me that you and the other two had already agreed; said I was the hold-out."

Brent shrugged as if he couldn't care less what Marcus said.

"I don't plan to let that guy goad me into saying something I might regret. I don't know who his followers are, but I'm not a fan. I don't think his so-called publicity would do any of us any favors, either."

He looked over at his café. "Besides, I'm shut down for this whole weekend, so I've lost that bump in business which I'll never recoup. I'm only hoping I'll get my boat in a prominent spot at the Misty Marina. A big for sale sign on it might spur someone to say, hey, that's exactly what I need. I need the cash." He added more to himself than for our benefit.

Maggie and I gave each other a knowing glance.

"Yeah," he continued, seemingly happy to unload all this angst on someone he thought was on his side. "Josie's folks gave us the boat. We said we didn't have time to use it and couldn't afford it. I guess they didn't want to deal with the headache of that money pit anymore and gave us the okay to sell it."

I suspected Maggie felt about two inches tall after hearing Brent's story of his boat, but at least she hadn't confronted him before learning this new detail. *That* would have been awkward.

"Any offers yet?" Luke asked.

"Are you interested? I'll give you a rock bottom price." Brent's hopeful tone told me he was pretty desperate to sell.

Luke glanced at me with his eyebrows raised. I could tell the lure of a boat appealed to him.

I shook my head, letting him know *I* wasn't interested.

"No," Luke answered, clearly disheartened. "I guess I don't have time, either."

I sighed with relief. We didn't need someone else's headache in our life.

Brent said, "When I got the call from Kyle that he was moving Wilhelmina's boat and we could have that spot, I was probably way more excited than I should have been. It seemed that one small thing *finally* went in our favor. But we'll have the mooring fees until it sells, so unless we unload it quickly, we'll have another setback."

"Do you know who your boat neighbor is?" I asked. It sounded like he was committed to that spot, but I had more bad news for him.

"Nope. Why?"

"Do you like surprises or do you like to be prepared?" I asked.

"I'm like a boy scout—always be prepared as much as possible. Who is it?"

"Marcus Willoby."

"You've got to be kidding! Of all the people that have boats at Misty Marina, why do I have to get stuck next to that guy?"

Brent, obviously distressed by this information, ran his fingers through his hair making it more unruly than ever.

"I hope he keeps to himself and doesn't annoy me with stupid suggestions about how I should run my café. Or worse, asking me for one of my special recipes. He'd have the gall to do that, too."

I patted Brent on the back. "At least now you won't be blind-sided. I suggest you ignore him like I will. That will get under his skin pretty quickly. He thrives on confrontation."

"I can do ignore like a champ." Brent even managed a half-grin after that comment.

I chuckled at the unexpected bright note in our conversation. "Listen, Brent," I said, not really sure how to approach this next question except straight on. "I heard that Wilhelmina had some business at your café last night around nine. Do you know anything about that?"

"Where'd you hear that?" His tone quickly turned to suspicion and anger again as he glanced at Maggie.

"It doesn't matter. But it might provide some information about who murdered Wilhelmina."

Maggie took Brent's arm firmly in hers. "Brent? Let's head back to your place now and figure out our next step."

She didn't have to ask twice. Brent jumped at the opportunity and moved quickly away from us, completely ignoring my question. Before Maggie followed him, she turned to me. "Want to hang out with me Sunday night?"

"It's your birthday. Aren't you doing something with AJ?" I asked, hoping I sounded sincere.

"Naw. He has to work." Her voice suggested a reluctant acceptance to an unwelcome situation. I felt bad, but it made my job of getting her to Sea Breeze easier.

"Well, sure. How about I pick you up around six with a surprise to make you forget all about AJ."

Maggie's unhappiness vanished. "Now that sounds more like my kind of celebration. Otherwise, I'd be sitting in my apartment with my kitty twiddling my thumbs." She jogged to catch up with Brent.

That went easier than I'd expected. But I did wonder how Maggie would take this big birthday surprise that would be waiting like an ambush at Sea Breeze.

"Brent has a mountain of troubles," Luke said, pulling me from my thoughts after we were alone.

"That he does."

The question remained: what had happened in the Savory Soup & Sandwich Café last night?

21

I had two more people to talk to before heading to Sea Breeze to see what Lily and Sue Ellen had cooked up for Maggie's surprise party.

And I wasn't looking forward to those conversations.

"Shall we walk to Hidden Treasures?" I asked Luke. Pip heard me say walk and darted ahead of us, prancing down the sidewalk.

"Were you asking me or Pip?" he laughed as we both followed behind her.

"You, actually, but I don't think we have much of a choice. Pip is already zeroed in on some great smell." She trotted in front of us with her nose to the ground, pulling me forward with her bandana flapping in the breeze.

"So, John Harmon," Luke said. "I haven't heard you say too much about him yet. Did Wilhelmina have him on her radar, too?"

"Oh, yeah. She hated all the cheap plastic stuff he sells at Hidden Treasures. When I talked to Chad in the kitchen after we finished lunch at the diner, he said that Wilhelmina had dumped a lot of trash on his doorstep. I suppose that isn't as big a motive to kill her as Larry or Brent had, but still, she was a thorn in his side."

Luke and I picked up our pace to keep up with Pip. "I've been wondering about this focus on the trash, Dani. Do folks really throw so much stuff on the beach and in Blueberry Bay as Wilhelmina ranted about?"

Luke glanced at the glimmering ocean that peeked between two buildings, with boats bobbing, seagulls soaring, and the continuous sound of the waves crashing on the beach. "I just find it hard to believe that people would be so careless."

"That's a really good question. Kyle said that Wilhelmina lied about Larry throwing trash overboard so maybe she cooked up this whole problem, so she had something to give purpose to her life. That would be sad."

Pip darted after a squirrel that had foolishly tried to carry a piece of bread off the sidewalk. The leash pulled her up short and the squirrel disappeared up a tree, scolding us the whole time.

"Come on Pip. The squirrel is cleaning up someone's bit of bread so it's a win-win for everyone." I reached out and latched onto Luke's arm. "That gives me an idea."

"Okay. We'll scour the sidewalk for snacks?"

"Come on. Don't be silly." I fanned my hands across the sky. "I'll call it: Beautiful Blueberry Bay. It's so simple. Rose already dedicated her latest article to Wilhelmina's vision of a trash-free bay. I'll take it one step further."

I felt giddy as the whole plan came into place in my head.

"So, what's the secret?"

"Lobster shaped trash cans. Something that symbolizes the beauty we're trying to protect. Businesses in town can sponsor a container, which means they pay for it and make sure it's always clean. No cost for the town and the trash problem…" I snapped my fingers for emphasis, "gone."

"You know Dani, that makes a lot of sense. Why

haven't we had more trash cans in place before now?"

I shrugged, wondering about that myself. "Maybe we get distracted with the arguments instead of working together to solve the problem with a simple solution. Plus, having cute trash receptacles will catch peoples' attention more than the traditional ones."

Luke turned to me with one of his heart-melting smiles. "And with the sponsor's name on each lobster it will provide a little advertising for that business, and at the same time, ensure they'll care for them properly."

Luke stopped and turned me to face him. "I'm marrying a genius. And on top of that, I'll work on the design and Blueberry Acres will sponsor the first Lobster Trash Trap in town. How about that?"

"I love it, Luke! Lobster Trash Trap is the *perfect* name." I jumped into his arms, almost knocking him over.

Pip barked and jumped up too, never wanting to be left out of a fun time.

"What's going on here?"

"Rose?" We almost knocked my grandmother over. In our enthusiasm for my idea, we didn't see her hurrying toward us.

"Hi, Rose," I said, "Luke and I have just come up with a solution to Wilhelmina's war on trash. At least something good will come out of this tragedy. You'll love this idea."

"I can't wait to hear all about it. At Sea Breeze. Didn't you get Sue Ellen's message?"

I pulled my phone out. "Oh. My battery's dead." I looked at Rose. Her floppy straw hat clutched in her hand and her sunglasses askew. A worried look darkened her face.

"Don't scare me, Rose. Is something wrong?" A lump choked me like a whole lobster tail got stuck on the way down.

She grabbed my arm. "It's Lily."

Time stopped for a moment. "What do you mean, it's Lily?"

"Come on, Danielle. We have to go to Sea Breeze. Right now."

Luke took my other arm. Somehow, I ended up in Rose's Cadillac with Pip on my lap. Instead of putting her paws on the dashboard as she always did, she must have sensed my fear and snuggled against my chest.

"I'll follow in your MG," Luke said, riffling through my bag for my keys.

I nodded, barely able to manage that much through a numbness that had taken over.

What happened to Lily?

Why wasn't Rose telling me anything?

"Someone ambushed her when she went out to get something from the car," Rose said, breaking the painful silence.

My arms tightened around Pip, but she didn't wiggle to get away. "Is she hurt?" As soon as the words left my mouth, I wasn't sure I wanted to know the answer.

Rose just focused on her driving for now.

We drove in this silence that wrenched my heart. Poor Lily. Had *I* put her in some kind of danger with all of my questions about Wilhelmina's murder?

"Danielle?" Rose's voice, normally strong and in control, quivered. "When you didn't answer your phone, I thought…"

"I'm so sorry I worried you." I could only imagine what had bombarded Rose's thoughts when she couldn't reach me, each option worse than the previous one because that's what our mind does when we let it fall into the what-if hole.

Like mine was doing right now as I thought about Lily.

My best forever friend. I'd fight for her if necessary, and I hadn't been at her side when she needed help. Or worse, whoever attacked her could have mistaken Lily for me.

Rose reached across the seat and held my hand. "Lily will be okay. Sue Ellen has her on the couch with ice on her bump."

The twisty road to Sea Breeze never felt so long and windy. "Go faster, Rose," I urged my grandmother who always obeyed the speed limit.

She did, screeching around the curves like a racecar driver.

Finally, Sea Breeze came into view. Normally my sanctuary, but today? I dreaded what I'd find inside.

Rose slammed the Cadillac into park.

What would we find inside?

22

I ran into Sea Breeze with Pip streaking ahead straight to Lily. I couldn't tell much when I first saw her stretched out on Rose's couch, but my amazing terrier knew Lily needed her special brand of doggie comfort. That was Pip's magic touch—always giving exactly what was needed.

"Lil," I said as I crouched next to the couch and hugged my friend. "What happened?"

Sue Ellen, like a mother hen, clucked and fussed with the ice pack on Lily's head and said, "It should have been me outside getting the last bag of groceries out of my car."

"I'll be fine, Sue Ellen. Stop beating yourself up. It's only a little bump."

I tenderly sifted my fingers over Lily's head to feel this 'little bump' for myself. "That's a *mountain*, Lil. Who did this?"

Anger surged through me replacing the fear I had from the moment Rose told me someone had ambushed Lily.

Lily stroked Pip, snuggling next to her.

"I wish I knew," she said in a voice too weak for my liking. "But I can't remember a thing. One minute I was pulling Sue Ellen's car door open and the next... she was kneeling next to me with a worried expression like she'd lost her giant leather tote bag or something equally devastating."

I appreciated Lily's attempt at a joke, but it didn't help much.

Rose, all business, with her glasses dangling from the chain around her neck, marched into the living room carrying a silver tray. I was impressed at the way she'd pulled herself together since she dragged me into her Cadillac looking like she'd been through a storm. "This calls for tea and chocolate truffles. Can you sit up, Lily?"

I helped Lily lean forward while Sue Ellen stuffed a couple of pillows behind her back for support.

Pip didn't budge. Well, she did wiggle a bit to get even closer to the patient before settling again with her head on Lily's lap.

"Now," Rose said, as she set a cup of tea on a small table next to Lily. "Let's talk about the plans for Maggie's surprise birthday party. What have you come up with so far, Sue Ellen?"

What? Who cared about a party when we needed to figure out who hurt Lily? I wanted to grill her to try and make her remember *something* about her attacker, but Rose gave me her leave-her-alone glare, so I zipped my lips closed.

"Well," Sue Ellen said, back in her favorite element—the center of attention. "We have a list of food planned, plus we thought Dani could share some of her blueberry cordial for this big event." She said it as a suggestion, but I took it as an order.

"Sure, but Maggie might need something stronger, as well. She's upset that AJ is working and asked if I'd do something with her Sunday night. It was hard to keep a straight face and not let the secret slip out."

That got a chuckle from Lily. "Seriously? Please don't make me laugh since it makes my head pound."

"Sorry, Lil. Anyway, I told her I'd pick her up at six and have a fun surprise planned. She's excited, and I got the impression that she thinks AJ's a loser."

"The problem is," Rose said, "he told her he had to work, and now he probably does, which will make him look like a heel if we put on this great party and he doesn't show up."

I fanned the air to dismiss their worries. "AJ promised me he'd be here, even if it's only to shout *surprise*." I blew on my tea and took a sip to test the temperature. Perfect. "Maggie's gonna wet her pants with this surprise. Either that or ring AJ's neck."

"That might be raising your expectations too high, Dani," Luke said. "You never know what will happen when you plan a surprise for someone. She might love it."

The twinkle in his eyes made me wonder if there was something I was missing about this whole affair. I shrugged it off since there was too much else to think about at the moment—Lily's well-being at the top of the list. I'd already taken care of my job. I'd arranged to pick up Maggie, and I'd get her to Sea Breeze.

The front door opened, and a familiar call broke

up our discussion. "Don't get up. I can let myself in," Maggie yelled as she walked toward the living room. Pip, taking her comfort job very seriously, stayed nestled next to Lily, not budging to say hello.

Maggie looked at all of us, hands on hips, telegraphing she was ready for action from the expression on her face.

"What happened, Lily?" All business, she moved into the room and pulled a chair close to the patient. "Sue Ellen texted me that someone mugged you? Right here at Sea Breeze?" She took Lily's hand. "Tell me everything you remember."

"She doesn't remember anything," I said, hoping to save Lily from a headache-inducing interrogation.

"Actually, I just remembered something," Lily said, squeezing her hands against her temples.

As one, we all leaned forward in eager antic-ipation.

"I heard footsteps, but thought it was Sue Ellen coming out to help me, so I didn't turn around. Then…"

"What, Lil?" I asked.

"I'm not sure, but I heard a voice. A man's voice. The only word I can remember is, trouble." Her arms fell back to her sides, and she shook her head.

She looked at me with a woeful expression. "Sorry, nothing else is coming back."

"Maybe someone is in trouble? Or, you're making trouble?" I suggested. "I wonder if that man thought you were me, Lil. He was—"

Lily twisted so she could face all of us. "I remember! He said, 'your friend is trouble.' That was the message. And then he pushed me. I don't think he wanted to hurt me, just prevent me from seeing who he was."

"So," Maggie asked, "you didn't see *anything*?"

Lily shook her head. "Nothing. It happened so fast it was over before anything even registered. What about you, Sue Ellen?"

"I heard tires screeching, but I didn't see anything, either. I suppose I should have run to the road to see what kind of car it was, but I was too worried when I saw Lily on the ground next to my car."

"Of course," Maggie soothed. "You did the right thing. Staying with Lily and calling for help. Just for a starting point, let's make a list of who might have warned Lily that Dani is trouble."

She looked at all of us in anticipation, waiting with pencil poised over her notebook.

"She could have meant Sue Ellen or Rose was

trouble," I said a bit defensively. "It might not have been *me* that the person was referring to."

"Really, Dani?" Luke said with unmistakable frustration in his voice. "Did you already forget that you got a couple of threats today?"

"What threats?" Maggie asked, giving me her don't hide anything look.

Great. Now everyone was going to give me a hard time about not keeping a low profile.

"Larry confronted us about the award ceremony change," Rose said to jog my memory in case I'd forgotten. I hadn't. "And if I recall properly, you also goaded him by mentioning how he'd be able to get a bigger boat now that Wilhelmina was dead."

"And don't forget that Marcus was angry about the change too, and said you'd be sorry," Luke added.

"He's probably got some blog ready to bash the Little Dog Diner or something like that. I didn't get the feeling his threat was physical in nature."

"Okay," Maggie said. "What you're saying is that Larry threatened Dani. He might also have ambushed Lily as a warning for her to think twice before she finds herself in trouble. And, Marcus also directed his anger at Dani."

Yeah, that summed it up, I thought.

Maggie's phone beeped with a text message. After she'd read it, she looked at the rest of us with something that she didn't often show—shock. "Someone just torched Marcus Willoby's boat. AJ's checking to make sure we're all okay."

There was a madman loose in Misty Harbor.

Where would he strike next?

23

*P*ip and I took an extra early run on the beach Saturday morning. Much to Pip's dismay, it was even too early for much seagull activity.

When we returned to Sea Breeze, Rose, ready for the day in a dark blue skirt and cream-colored cashmere sweater, informed me that she was heading into town with us. "With all this nonsense going on, I have no intention of leaving you alone at the Little Dog Diner, Danielle. I'd be here worrying myself to death, so, don't even think about arguing."

"I can use the help," I said, much to her surprise. Sit was obvious that she expected some push back from me. "If we get everything prepared for the day, Chad and Christy can take over."

"Now, don't think you can leave them with all the work so you can go sticking your nose into everyone's business. Haven't you learned *anything*, Danielle?" Rose's best I've-learned-so-much-in-my-long-life expression dared me to back down or I'd be on her bad side for the rest of the day.

"As a matter of fact, I learned from the best. Stay strong, be smart, and don't back down." I was referring to one of the many life lesson's Rose had instilled in me over the years I'd lived with her. She hated it when I used her own words against her, but it was oh, so satisfying for me and I couldn't stop the grin that grew on my face.

Rose tried her hardest to keep a stern look in place, but after I counted silently to three, she laughed and hugged me. "I'm thankful you've been listening to me and *something* seeped through that tangled mess of auburn curls. Now, let's get this show on the road."

I wasn't exactly sure what she meant by that, but what I did know was that Rose probably would make sure someone was always with me until we had solved this latest mystery. I had Pip though, and I liked to think that the two of us could solve any problem.

Time would tell how that would play out.

So, with Rose's floppy hat in place, Pip's orange with fall leaves bandana tied neatly around her neck, and me with my determination to look anything straight on, we slid into the MG and headed into Misty Harbor.

If nothing else, the Little Dog Diner made me smile with its bright white siding and red trim appeal. Nestled between two historical buildings, it invited locals and tourists to please come in, relax, and enjoy some traditional Maine culinary dishes.

I pulled into the narrow driveway between the diner and Rose's Blueberry Bay Grapevine office. I glanced up at the darkened windows in the apartment above her office where Maggie lived, but saw no sign of life.

"You go ahead inside. I'll take Pip for a quick walk around so she can get any new smells taken care of before she settles down in my office," I said to Rose.

"Don't be long, or I'll send the cavalry after you." She tossed her straw hat on the passenger seat, grabbed her big hobo bag, and let herself in through the side door of the diner.

Since it was so early still, I didn't bother with Pip's leash. With her nose to the ground, she followed some trail that I wished I could follow, too.

Instead, I stood quietly listening to the waves and the clanging of the bells on the navigational buoys. Overhead, the seagulls soared, keeping a watchful eye on all the activity below.

I loved Misty Harbor and Blueberry Bay. I wouldn't trade it for a million dollars.

"Dani?"

I shrieked at the sudden intrusion into my solitude. "Larry? What are you doing here so early?" My heart skipped a couple of beats. What did I expect? He'd recently threatened me, and I had no backup. I stepped back and whistled for Pip, praying she hadn't wandered too far away.

"I was hoping to find you before you got too busy," he said. "It's about Marcus Willoby." I backed away, but Larry stepped closer to me.

Pip ran to my side and barked her warning at the intruder.

Larry reached out and grabbed my arm.

I flinched.

Pip growled and charged at Larry.

He dropped his hand. "Sorry. I completely understand your wariness around me. I want to apologize about yesterday. Not that there's any excuse for my behavior, but I was upset and angry.

Believe me when I say, in light of all that's happened, my choice of words was appalling."

He hung his head and kicked at a stone with the toe of his boat shoe. "Being upset is no excuse for taking my anger out on you.

"Okay." The least I could do was hear him out. "Let's go inside and discuss Marcus over coffee." That way, it would be Rose, Pip, and me against Larry if he'd come for some nefarious reason.

"I was hoping that's what you'd say." His smile actually softened his face enough to make him look handsome *if* you liked the sun-weathered craggy-lined look.

"You have the best coffee in town," he said. And, with pleading eyes, he added, "I wouldn't mind a muffin to go with it if I could buy one before you're officially open for business."

I followed Larry through the side door that Rose had left unlocked for me. Coffee aroma hit me along with a sweet scent of cinnamon and sugar.

"I have tea for you and coffee for me, Dani," Rose said over her shoulder. She hadn't turned around yet and noticed I wasn't alone.

When she did, she said, "Oh… company. Hello, Larry. What are *you* doing here?"

"Apologizing," he answered. "And talking about Marcus. Mind if I join you two lovely ladies?"

"Three," I said pointing to Pip. She still regarded Larry with suspicion.

He nodded to Pip but didn't talk to her. I had to assume he wasn't a dog person. I never completely trusted anyone who didn't like animals.

"Take a seat at the counter, Larry. Coffee?" Rose asked.

"Yes please, and a muffin if you'd be so kind."

"What's up with Marcus?" I moved behind the counter so I could mix up the morning's pancake batter while we talked. I couldn't figure out why he was being such a nice guy. He had to have a motive.

"You really shouldn't do that interview with Marcus," he said. Nothing like getting to the point. "I talked to John and Brent and neither of them are interested. Why did you agree to it? Marcus loves to stir up controversy for that blog of his. He's nothing but a troublemaker."

"I'm *not* doing it. Did he tell you I was?"

"He did." Larry bit into the apple spice muffin Rose had placed in front of him along with a cup of coffee.

"Delicious," he said before continuing. "The apple chunks add a nice tart surprise."

"Who do you think tried to burn up his boat?" I asked hoping for a shock factor.

Crumbs flew out of Larry's mouth as he choked and reached for his coffee. "What?" he asked once he'd managed to wash down the chunks of muffin.

"You didn't hear? Someone started a fire on his boat," Rose repeated. "Fortunately, it was quickly contained, and his boat only suffered minor damage."

"Ha! He probably did it himself, so he'd have material for his blog."

"Seriously? You think he'd torch his own boat?" Rose said. That sounded ridiculous even by Marcus's standards.

"No, not really. But who *would* pull that kind of stunt? The whole marina could have gone up in flames. Maybe someone sent it as a warning or something like that for Marcus to change the focus of his blog."

That was a loaded comment, especially coming on the heels of the warning Lily received.

"So, Larry, there's a lot of evidence pointing toward Brent as Wilhelmina's murderer. Do *you* think he killed her?" I was curious to know who he'd try to incriminate.

With one elbow on the counter, Larry thoughtfully sipped his coffee. "Brent had a lot to gain with her dead, but I'm not going to speculate. He's a fellow businessman, and this whole bizarre situation has made me realize that we should all work together. You know, Dani, I'd love to recommend the Little Dog Diner to my tour customers. If you want, I could hang a menu on the boat if you would promote my tours in here somewhere." He looked around the diner. "I've even considered a discount coupon. You could leave a stack next to your cash register. What do you think?"

"It's an interesting idea. I'll think about it." I wasn't sure I trusted this new and improved Larry Sidwell. Sure, he apologized for his threatening behavior, but was it only so he could get my endorsement for his tour business?

Larry finished the last of his coffee and slid a five-dollar bill under his cup. "Thanks for listening to me. By the way, how's Lily?"

A frosty stream surged through my veins. "Lily? Why do you ask?" My voice sounded normal to my ears even if I was reeling inside. Did Larry know about Lily's attack? Had he ambushed her before he set fire to Marcus's boat?

"Oh, no reason. It's just that I miss seeing her here working with you."

With that, Larry walked out the side door.

I looked at Rose who stared at the closed door.

"Was *that* the real reason why Larry came here? To ask about Lily?" I asked Rose.

"An odd question for sure," Rose answered. "I don't trust him one bit."

"Me neither."

24

The side door of the Little Dog Diner squeaked.

I looked at it and then at Rose, my heart still pounding from Larry's exit.

My stomach twisted in a knot.

Was he returning? Was his apology all a joke, and he had more threats up his sleeve?

Or, had he sized us up and decided we were no match for him, and he'd take us out before Misty Harbor woke up?

Fortunately, before my thoughts sank any lower, Maggie walked in.

With her gray kitten, Radar, nestled in her arms.

"Awww," I said. My tension drained away in a

flash at the sight of this adorable, playful, ball of silky fur.

"You haven't seen Radar in so long, I figured it's early enough for a quick visit." Maggie dropped the fur ball into my arms. "Enjoy!"

I buried my cheek in Radar's kitteny softness. "I plan to. Come here, Pip. See what I've got." I crouched down so Pip could see the newcomer. She kept her distance though, not sure if this one was as ornery as Trouble.

Radar reached her paw out to Pip. The Pipster sniffed tentatively and when no claws met her nose, she bowed down playfully. The kitten leaped from my arms and circled in and out through Pip's legs, rubbing against her new friend.

"Perfect. I've found a babysitter," Maggie said gleefully. "I hate when I have to leave her in the apartment all day. Maybe she could have a play date at Sea Breeze?"

"I'm not sure how Trouble will like it," I said.

"Oh, pshaw." Rose waved her hand dismissively. "Trouble can take it or leave it. He doesn't make the decisions around there, and it's better if he understands the hierarchy sooner rather than later."

"Well, that's good to hear," I said as I cuddled

Radar again. "Pip and I were under the impression that we were second class citizens now."

"Trouble's all talk. Don't let him bully you."

Easier with people than animals, I thought to myself. The four-legged types always zeroed in on my soft spot.

Maggie poured herself a large mug of coffee. "Lily told me to let you know that she's feeling fine today. She still has a bump but no headache. I think she's got something planned with Sue Ellen, today but she didn't give me any details."

Of course, she didn't want to share details and risk ruining Maggie's surprise birthday party. "Thanks for letting her stay with you last night. I guess she didn't feel comfortable spending the night at Sea Breeze after getting whacked on her head. I can't blame her," I said.

"Did you have a customer already this morning? I thought I heard a man's voice."

"We did, and I can't figure out his motive. I was waiting outside with Pip after we got here, and Larry surprised me. He said he came to apologize for his remarks yesterday that, in my mind, amounted to a threat."

"But?" Maggie looked at me over the rim of her coffee cup.

"As he was leaving, he asked us how Lily was."

Maggie's coffee mug landed on the counter with a thud. "Was he referring to her whack on the head?"

"That's the mystery," Rose said. "Larry claimed he only meant he missed seeing her working here at the diner with Dani. But it was such a strange random comment."

"Maybe he was fishing to find out if Lily remembered anything about the attack."

"All I know," Rose said, "is that Larry Sidwell is a slippery businessman and everything he does is to benefit himself."

"Like the tour promotion he wants me to do?" Now that I had some time to think about it, I had second thoughts about promoting him. "When he mentioned it, he was all like—let's work together, it will be good for everyone. Until now, I'd forgotten that he sells gourmet boxed meals on his tours, so why would he recommend the Little Dog Diner?"

Maggie leaned over the glass pastry display. "Any chance I could trouble you for one of those blueberry turnovers? Fruit is healthy, right?"

I chose the plumpest turnover for Maggie but didn't tell her dessert didn't qualify as health food. "How's it going with you and AJ?" I knew this might be a difficult question, but I wanted to know if he'd let any details about the investigation slip out.

"Funny you ask." She bit off a third of the turnover, letting gobs of squished blueberries drip down her chin.

"Oops," she said and grabbed a napkin to mop up the mess before it stained her white t-shirt, then swiveled around on the counter stool. "He sounded a little sad when I told him you were taking me out for my birthday."

"I'm sure he's sad to miss it, but he'll make it up another night, don't you think?"

"There's only one day when I turn thirty, so another day just won't be the same." She sounded wistful, and I actually felt kind of bad for her that she had to go through this. I consoled myself with the thought that it would make the surprise that much better.

"And he told me he's looking at three people who might have started the fire at the marina."

"He shared that information? That's progress." I said. "Who's on his list of suspects?"

"Don't expect a miracle, Dani. He didn't give me the names."

"Oh. Of course, it wouldn't be that easy. Rose, which three people would you pick?"

"I hate to think of *anyone* who might start a fire as a warning... or worse. But when someone is desperate, who knows what they might do? I suppose Kyle or his father might have a good reason to rid themselves of Marcus so he wouldn't spread bad publicity about the marina. Or, your three contenders for the Best Business Award might do it in an attempt to keep him from any more business-bashing in town. It's a serious warning, for sure."

This was all too depressing. "Warning about what?" I asked. "It doesn't make sense to me. What happened to talking instead of setting fires and bashing people over the head?"

Rose leaned on the counter and looked across the room thoughtfully. "A lot of people are fed up with how Marcus is portraying Misty Harbor, if you ask me. He magnifies problems without adding anything about all the wonderful events and busi-nesses we have here. You know, in some respects, he's worse than Wilhelmina. At least she had Misty Harbor and Blueberry Bay in her best interest, even if she didn't handle her complaints tactfully. So, to answer your question, Danielle, maybe someone wants him to back off on his blog."

I hadn't connected Wilhelmina and Marcus as two of the town villains.

Wilhelmina's protests definitely hurt local businesses. Marcus damaged Misty Harbor with his negative perspectives. If someone sent a warning through Lily for me to keep my mouth shut, it wasn't such a huge leap to imagine that same person warning Marcus to keep quiet.

Would they resort to a more drastic measure next to silence me for good?

25

I couldn't have been happier to see Chad and Christy arrive at the Little Dog Diner. Their smiling faces lightened the somber mood. If I wanted to, I could leave the diner in their capable hands.

After much oohing and aahing over Radar, Chad disappeared into the kitchen. Christy began the morning check of all the booths, filling napkin dispensers, refilling the sugar bowls, and straightening the settings on the tables where necessary.

Rose left with Pip for her office next door, and Maggie took Radar back to her apartment, plus a bag with hot tea and an egg sandwich for Lily.

It had been a whirlwind morning, and the diner hadn't even opened yet.

I glanced out the window as Misty Harbor began a new day and wondered what was headed in my direction. The answer came striding toward me as AJ approached up the walk with a determined gait. Apparently, I wouldn't even have this last ten minutes before we opened for business with some peace.

I opened the front door instead of leaving AJ outside to attract unwanted attention. If people saw him in his uniform on the diner doorstep, it would arouse suspicion. The last thing I needed right now was rumors spreading about the diner, given all the drama going on.

AJ tipped his cap. "Morning, Dani. Okay if I come in for a few minutes before you officially open for the day?"

I considered saying no, but what choice did I have? Besides, if I cooperated, maybe I'd learn something important. I stepped to one side and waited for him to enter.

"What can I do for you, AJ? Coffee?"

"Please. Extra-large after the night I had, and I might even need a refill." He sat at the counter with his hat on his lap.

I fixed his coffee with extra cream and no sugar

before I dared ask him a question. "Here you go," I said, adding an apple spice muffin as an extra, soften-him-up, sweet bribe.

"You know what I love about this place?" he asked. "Your coffee. It's always hot, strong, and you don't have all those fancy flavors that have become so popular."

I really didn't have time for small talk. "Have you figured out anything about the fire at the marina yet?" I asked, deciding it was now or never to get anything out of him before the regular customers invaded the diner.

"Nothing. It's as if some invisible force floated over the town disrupting everything. Seriously. I've got ideas but no evidence."

"Larry suggested that Marcus set it himself. What about that theory?"

"Believe me, I've considered everything, but there's nothing that puts him at his boat when the fire started. As a matter of fact, Kyle saw him drive into the marina, and they both noticed the smoke at the same time."

"Maybe it was just an accident," I suggested.

"Maybe," AJ said without much enthusiasm. He didn't have to say the words out loud, but I could tell that he suspected foul play. "This whole weekend has been nothing but me chasing one disaster after another. Everything leads nowhere."

He bit into the muffin like he was taking his frustration out on the plump treat. I hoped it helped his mood.

"I had a strange conversation with Larry this morning," I said. Nothing like adding more confusion to the situation, but it was something that might help AJ.

"Don't get me started on him. All he does is moan and complain about how I postponed the award ceremony. The way he talks, you'd think his business is about to sink if he doesn't get an influx of customers. I think he's just greedy." He took another bite of the muffin followed by a swallow of coffee.

I folded my arms on the counter and leaned in so no one would hear me. "Larry came in this morning all friendly and apologetic," I said.

"What for?" AJ asked. I could tell I had his attention, as he put the muffin down and looked in my eyes.

"For what he said to me yesterday. Then he asked me to promote his tours. Of course, he said he'd recommend the Little Dog Diner to his customers." I wondered if AJ would catch the sarcasm in my voice.

He titled his head in surprise. "I've never known Larry to help someone who wasn't named Larry Sidwell. I don't mean to badmouth any business in town, Dani, but if I were you, I'd think long and hard before I got involved with him."

"It didn't take me more than two winks to make up my mind about that proposal." I winked at AJ to show him exactly how much time I spent thinking.

At least that brought a grin to his face.

"You know," I said, "if his business is doing so badly, he might be really desperate for that bigger tour boat. More space plus more customers equals more money." I wasn't exactly being subtle with my suggestion.

"He has about as good a motive as anyone, but I need hard evidence. Can you remember anything at *all* from the time you followed Pip to the café and discovered Wilhelmina—people, cars, noises— anything at all?"

I thought back to early Friday morning. Main Street had been quiet when I drove in with Pip. "I didn't notice anything, but Pip sure did because she shot out of my car like a little torpedo. Sorry, I can't help more. You know what worries me, AJ?"

"What?"

"The other problems. Lily's ambush and the fire on Marcus's boat. Do you think it's all connected to Wilhelmina's murder? It's like you never know when the next creepy incident will pop up."

AJ pursed his lips. Then, he drained his coffee cup. "I wish I knew for sure but I'm going on the assumption that everything is connected. I need to find the missing link in this chaos." He tapped the counter before he stood up. "Thanks for the coffee and muffin. I owe you for that. And thanks for letting me in early so I could enjoy the refreshments in peace."

"Sure, AJ. Anytime."

He smoothed his hair and positioned his baseball cap on his head. "Everyone wants to ask me when I'll catch the killer. Don't they realize that if I could answer *that* question, I'd have the killer locked up already?"

"People are worried. It's natural they want everything back to normal. By the way, how's it going with Maggie? Is she talking to you?"

"Sort of." He grinned mischievously. "But it'll be

worth it to see her face tomorrow night. She's in for one whopper of a surprise."

"I hope you know what you're doing, AJ. You know, this could really backfire."

"Naw. I'm not worried."

Well, that made one of us.

26

*A*s soon as AJ left, I turned the *CLOSED* sign to *OPEN*. The door opened with a refreshing jingle and a few of the early regulars walked inside.

"What was the Detective doin' heah so early, Dani?" Joe, one of the local fishermen in town asked as he took his usual spot at the counter.

"Just avoiding you guys," I answered, giving him a pat on his back as I walked to the other side of the counter. "Your regular this morning?"

"Ayuh."

Joe's Maine accent always got a chuckle out of me. At least *I* knew what he meant. "Here you go, one steaming black coffee and two blueberry muffins. When will you ever try something different?"

"Nevah, Dani. I like supportin' Blueberry Acres."

I knew that was about all the talking I'd get out of Joe, so I left him to enjoy his morning ritual and discussion with the other regulars. I don't know how they managed but talking about the Maine weather forecast made up ninety percent of these old codgers' ruminations. The other ten percent probably revolved around Wilhelmina Joy. Unfortunately, it was all speculation and none of the hard facts that would help AJ.

I poked my head into the kitchen. "Everything under control back here?" I asked Chad.

He gave me a quick thumbs up before he slid two platters under the warming lights. He wiped his hands on his apron. "I talked to Brent last night about his café cleanup."

I moved closer to Chad and leaned my hip against the counter. "Has he started?"

"Not yet. I told him Christy and I could help, though, whenever he gets the go ahead from Detective Crenshaw."

I helped myself to a banana from the fruit bowl.

"How is he doing overall?" A wreck, I guessed, after what happened.

"My opinion? I think he's about ready to throw in the towel. He said this weekend should have been a busy and profitable couple of days and now he's not sure he wants to keep fighting to survive. It's sad. He's a good guy and a hard worker."

"What would he do instead?"

Chad shrugged. "He didn't say. I doubt he has a backup plan. No one goes into business with the expectation that it will crash and burn."

"Did he mention anything to you about meeting Wilhelmina at the café the night before she was murdered?"

Chad poured batter on the griddle. I busied myself dishing up bowls of sliced fruit to go with the pancake orders.

"He said it might have been the costliest decision he's ever made. Brent and Wilhelmina talked outside for about five minutes. He insisted she was alive and ornery when they parted ways. He thinks she was furious that he tried to pay her to stop her protest, and she broke into the café after he left."

"Why, though?"

"Well, the place was destroyed. Brent thinks she

was intent on teaching him a lesson and finishing off his business in one last major trashing."

"That doesn't bode well for Brent, does it? Maybe he circled back for some reason and found her inside and—"

"Brent didn't kill Wilhelmina." Chad's voice, usually even keeled, came out in a deep growl. "I'm sure he didn't. He's too honest to lie about something like that. Detective Crenshaw would see right through him in a heartbeat."

"But, who then?" In a town this small, someone should have seen something, but if they did, they weren't coming forward.

Chad turned around and looked at me with a hint of accusation in his eyes. "Who *else* benefits from the café closing?"

"You think *I* killed her?"

"No. Sorry. That's not what I meant. Maybe there's someone else in town who wants that spot for a new business, I don't know. Maybe someone just didn't like Brent. Or, maybe Wilhelmina was just in the wrong place at the wrong time and it's not about the Savory Soup & Sandwich Café at all."

"So, the question should be," I said trying to get to the very basics. "Who wanted Wilhelmina dead?"

"Yeah, that's the question, and unfortunately, it

points back to Brent." I could see in Chad's troubled eyes his obvious frustration that his friend was smack in the middle.

"And, Larry Sidwell," I said. With Wilhelmina blocking any expansion at the marina, Larry couldn't get a bigger tour boat. Now, he's free and clear."

"I never thought of that," Chad said. "I did hear him brag about how he's got a brand spanking new business model. He says he'll be bigger and better than ever next spring, especially if he wins the Best Business Award."

"But what about the fire on Marcus's boat? Why Larry would do that?" I asked.

Chad slid three fluffy pancakes onto a plate, and I added the fruit slices and an individual bottle of maple syrup. Customers always raved about the fact that the Little Dog Diner served nothing but real New England maple syrup.

Christy balanced the four plates and kicked open the swinging door.

"About that fire. Brent thought it might have been accidental, but with Marcus all freaking out about his boat and insisting someone was out to get him, Detective Crenshaw is being extra careful with his investigation."

"I suppose on top of the murder, Lily being ambushed, and the fire, it's hard to think anything is an accident anymore." I said.

"What happened to Lily?" Chad stopped flipping pancakes and looked at me like I'd just said the sky was falling.

I directed Chad's attention back to the grill, a reminder that pancakes can burn faster than a boat tied up at the marina.

"Oops, thank you," he said, plating them just in time.

"I guess you haven't heard, Chad. Someone ambushed Lily last night. Knocked her over and left her unconscious for a bit."

I rubbed my head thinking about the giant bump she'd received.

"Thankfully, she's okay today." If anything serious happened to Lily I'd never forgive myself. Especially since I believed the whole thing was a warning for me.

Chad took the next order from the carousel. "Is someone after *you* now, Dani? I mean, this seems to grow bigger every time I turn around." He added more bacon to the grill, talking while he worked. "It's more than just Wilhelmina and her protest. Who'll get targeted next, do you think?"

I stacked a few clean plates next to the grill to help out. "I don't know, but that's why I'm thankful you and Christy are such quick learners. I can leave the diner in your capable hands today. I have questions that need answers before something else happens."

"Are you sure that's what you should be doing? Let the police handle it."

I stood ready to help, but Chad had everything under control, flipping the bacon and adding the ingredients to the omelet while we tried to sort out the potential worries I faced.

"Detective Crenshaw told me he's running in circles, Chad. If I'm in the crosshairs of this creep, I don't plan to sit around twiddling my fingers. And don't worry, I'll let Maggie tag along." I smiled trying to convince him that I wouldn't do anything stupid to put myself in danger. "She's really good at the private eye stuff. I'll be in good hands."

"I know I can't stop you, but can I give you my unsolicited opinion?"

I nodded, wondering what Chad would say.

"When Brent talked to Wilhelmina the other night, she bragged about how proud she was that she was having such a big impact on the businesses in town—especially his café and Larry's tour company. She couldn't wait to see both of them fail. Be very wary of that slimy guy, Dani. I guess the police can't link Larry to the crimes, yet, but he's the kind of guy who wouldn't stop at anything to protect himself and his business."

Chad's words sent chills through me.

I had to figure out how to end the mayhem before someone else got hurt.

27

I loaded six pecan sticky buns into a bag and dashed up the stairs to Maggie's apartment. I needed to see for myself that Lily was really okay.

When I entered the living room, Radar darted between Pip's legs like she was playing hide and seek. Pip couldn't seem to figure out what the kitten was up to, but it sure was entertaining Lily, Maggie, and Rose.

"How are you feeling, Lil?" I asked after I greeted everyone and deposited my breakfast treat on the table.

She reached for the bump on her head, checked out the size, and said, "Just a small lump today, and it's only sore if I push on it."

I slapped her hand away. "Leave it alone then. Here, I brought you some sticky buns." I glanced at Maggie. "I know what kind of cook your hostess is."

Maggie threw up her hands like an overwhelmed worker. "I can't be brilliant at everything. Besides, I live next door to the best diner in Maine so why would I ever want to cook for myself?"

I loved her reasoning.

I flopped on the couch next to Lily. "Did you by any chance remember anything else from last night?"

"No, but I found this on the front seat of Sue Ellen's car when she dropped me off here last night." Lily handed a red plastic lobster to me.

"Where'd it come from?"

"Well," Rose said, "we've been trying to figure that out. It looks like something John sells at Hidden Treasures. He's got all kinds of plastic souvenirs, and Maggie's planning to ask him about it. I'll stay here with Lily."

Lily began to protest. "You—"

"It's not open for discussion, Lily." Rose tenderly smoothed a few loose blonde strands of hair out of Lily's face. "Someone needs to stay with you until that lump is gone. You don't mess with concussions."

"Rose is right, Lil," I said. The idea of Lil having a concussion almost made me want to cry. "You need to take it easy." I handed her laptop to her. "So just get comfy and enjoy your downtime, okay?"

She sighed as her shoulders drooped, and Lily opened her laptop. "If I must sit here, I'm going to check Marcus's blog." She gave me a wary look. "Have you checked it out yet?"

I shook my head. I hadn't had time… and I didn't want to feed his ego by adding another view to his blog, but I didn't stop myself from looking at Lily's screen with her. After all, it would still only count as one view so I managed a small virtual pat on my back.

"Whoa!" I said as I read the headline to myself.

Lily read it out loud. "*Four suspects in the Wilhelmina Joy-less murder.*"

I crowded as close as I could get to see the smaller print under the headline of his blog post. "*Four finalists for the Best Business Award in Misty Harbor—who did it? All benefit from the sad death of Wilhelmina Joy who you fondly know as my boat neighbor. Yes, someone in town took it upon him or herself to silence Wilhelmina's protests. And, you won't believe this, but now that person is also trying to silence me, Marcus Willoby, by setting fire to my beloved boat, Instigator. Fortunately, the fire only did minor damage and now my voice is stronger than ever. Together, let's get to the bottom of my boat neighbor's murder. Which business owner silenced Wilhelmina? The Little Dog Diner, the Savory Soup & Sandwich Café, the Hidden Treasures souvenir shop ... or ... last but not least, the Misty Harbor and Beyond Tour Company?*

Stay tuned for updates!

Lily snapped her laptop closed. "Enough of that! This reads like Marcus has turned Wilhelmina's murder into some sort of game. Next, he'll be taking bets."

"Maggie?" I said as I pushed myself off the couch. "I'd say it's time someone had a friendly little chat with John at Hidden Treasures. He's managed to keep a fairly low profile."

Maggie grinned with her this-is-what-I'm-good-at expression. "I couldn't agree more. From that scowl on your face, I'd say you're ready to find out what he has to say about his relationship with Wilhelmina and whether or not he knows how that plastic lobster ended up in Sue Ellen's car."

"Here." Rose handed the lobster to me. "You'd better bring the evidence. Not that I expect him to admit he dropped it like a calling card, but his face might reveal something."

"Oh, this reminds me. Luke and I have solved

the trash problem that Wilhelmina spent so much energy railing about without offering a solution."

"We're all ears. Do tell what you came up with," Rose said.

"The short story is we'll have businesses in town sponsor lobster shaped trash containers. And Luke came up with the perfect name." I couldn't be more proud of him.

"Trash and Bash?" Maggie said.

"No... Claw and Order," Lily shouted over Maggie.

"Not bad, but not even close to Lobster Trash Trap." I waited for their response.

"That's brilliant, Danielle!" Rose clapped her hands together. "How about the base is designed like a lobster trap with claws on either side to catch the trash?"

"Well, Luke is designing something, and he already signed on as the very first Lobster Trash Trap sponsor. Each sponsor pays for their trap, maintains it, and gets to advertise their business on it, too. Win-win, right?"

"A perfectly simple solution. Put me down for two—one for the Blueberry Bay Grapevine, and one for the Little Dog Diner."

"Hey, me too!" said Lily. "I need to get some advertising out there for my catering business.

"Maggie?" I looked at her wondering if she'd cough up money for a Lobster Trash Trap, too.

"Sure. Why not? It's for a good cause," she answered without much enthusiasm. I wondered what that was about but, knowing Maggie, she'd tell us when she was ready.

"Onward to Hidden Treasures," I said. "Come on, Pip. I think Radar needs a nap, and you need a walk."

"Wait a minute," Rose said as she dug around in her hobo bag. "I found this new bandana for her, and I think it's appropriate today." She tied on a hot pink bandana covered with silver *Best Dog* medals. "There you go, just in case someone doesn't already know this."

Pip sat quietly as if she was giving us all a chance to admire her new attire. She was an attention hog, but in a good way.

Radar reached up with a paw and batted the corner of the bandana.

"She wants one, too," Maggie said. "In miniature, though."

"No worries." Rose pulled out another hot pink bandana, about a quarter of the size of Pip's with

Best Kitten on the silver medals. "There. Now, Pip and Radar are sisters from another mother."

"AJ's gonna hate it when he sees Radar wearing that bandana," Maggie said with a sly grin. "Please don't tell him where you got it, Rose, or else he'll get one for his kitty, and we all know that there's only one best kitty in Misty Harbor."

Their competition thing made me wonder if Maggie was worried what AJ would think of her Lobster Trash Trap advertising her PI business.

I opened the door for Pip and Maggie and followed them out.

I hoped we'd learn something useful from John at Hidden Treasures, but I had a worried feeling in my stomach.

Tourists strolled along Main Street in Misty Harbor, window-shopping, and, from what I could tell, generally enjoying the lovely October day.

Everything appeared normal, but I knew otherwise.

"I can't advertise my PI business on the Lobster Trash Trap," Maggie said as we made our way to Hidden Treasures.

"You don't have to." Finally, she was talking about her problem.

She let out a deep sigh that sounded like a balloon losing its air. "Oh, good. AJ would pop an artery. It's bad enough that I get jobs that he says interfere with his police work, but if I advertise, he'd think I was completely undermining him."

"Don't worry about it, Maggie. You can sponsor the trash trap, and we'll figure out some other way to label it. The main thing is for business owners to maintain them and help keep the town clean."

"I can do that part with my eyes closed." She grabbed my arm, pulling me to a sudden stop in front of Hidden Treasures. The other people on the sidewalk had to swerve around us, but Maggie was oblivious. "I've got the perfect solution. I'll dedicate mine to Wilhelmina."

"Yeah," I said, trying to regain my equilibrium. "That's a great idea. Maybe every container should have some kind of tribute to her memory. We can figure that out later." At last Maggie unloaded that problem. Now we could focus on the really important issue… sorting out the murder before the culprit struck again.

Several people strolling by, stopped to admire Pip, even bending down to pet her. Most chuckled when they read her *Best Dog* bandana. One middle-aged woman even asked, "Is she the town mascot?"

I swelled with pride. "Pip? I suppose you could say that she's the unofficial town mascot. She spends a lot of time here while I'm working at the Little Dog Diner. Most of the locals know her."

"She sure is a cutie."

Of course, I agreed one hundred percent with that observation. "See how she's wagging her tail? She's saying thanks," I said with a laugh.

"The Little Dog Diner?" The woman straightened up and asked, as if some alarm bell had just gone off in her brain. "Didn't I hear that the owner of that place might be connected to the vicious murder of a sweet old lady? I wouldn't *dare* set foot in there, much less eat anything *she* cooked."

Sweet old lady? Before I had a chance to explain she had bad information and dispel her fears, she trotted off with her hand in the air, calling and waving to an acquaintance.

"That's the last thing I want to hear," I mumbled. "I need to set her straight."

I began to take after the woman, but Maggie pulled me up short and dragged me inside Hidden Treasures. "Our time is much better spent working on solving the crime instead of educating ignorant people who choose to believe rumors. Just let it go, Dani."

Even though Maggie was right, the woman's comment was like a punch in my gut. I vowed to get to the bottom of this mess before I lost more customers.

Maggie jabbed me in my side and tipped her head toward a big bin of red plastic lobsters in several sizes. "It matches the evidence left at the scene of the crime, if you ask me. Maybe we're getting closer to finding who ambushed Lily."

"Hello, ladies... and Pip," John said, coming out from behind the counter. He, at least, was a dog lover and allowed his customers to bring well-behaved dogs into his store. Dog weren't the threat to his souvenirs as much as many children were. Too many tempting items in a store like his to attract small fingers. But, from what I'd observed, he didn't seem to mind that, either, which showed his good customer relations, and the reason he was one of the finalists for the Best Business Award.

"Hi, John. How's business?" I asked.

Dressed like one of his tourist customers in plaid pants and an ocean blue polo shirt, he rocked his hand back and forth. "So-so," he said. "Not what I had hoped for, but it could be worse, considering."

"Considering what?" Maggie asked as she positioned several lobsters on her hand.

"Aren't they just the cutest lobsters?" he asked,

ignoring Maggie's question. I knew she wouldn't let him get away with it.

"Considering what, John?" She leaned right into his face. "Considering the impact of Wilhelmina's protest, her murder, or Marcus's blog?"

He sucked in an audible breath of air. "Let's move to a less busy part of the store. Customers can listen in here." He managed to whisper to us and at the same time smile and keep his eyes on a family browsing near us. I guessed he was afraid they'd leave without making a purchase.

He was right. The family, two parents and four unruly boys, bustled toward the door before they'd even looked at any of the souvenirs. "I don't wanna leave," one of the boys said and lurched toward a display of lobster boat replicas. Each parent lunged and grabbed the boy just in time before the whole rack tipped over. With all four boys firmly in hand, they exited into the sunshine.

"Oh, dear." John twisted his hands together in distress. "It's been like that all morning. I don't know what's going on."

"Maybe they left because their boys were about to destroy your displays and the parents didn't want to pay for any damage," I suggested. It was a distinct possibility. The point of all the kitschy stuff was to draw impulse purchases, but at the same time, all the tall shelves loaded to overflowing became a disaster waiting to happen.

Maggie, tapping a box of wooden matches on the palm of her hand, asked, "Why were you at the marina last night?"

Okay, that was a lightning speed change of subject and an interesting question, which I wasn't expecting. Did Maggie know something she hadn't shared about the fire on Marcus's boat?

John backed deeper into the rear of his store, and we had no choice but to follow if we wanted answers. "How did you know that? Brent said he wouldn't tell anyone."

Maggie, cool calm and collected, said, "A lucky guess. So, tell us why *you* were there?"

"To look at Brent's boat. He told me he was short on cash and he offered me a fantastic deal. So, I figured, what the heck, looking doesn't cost anything."

"Except it put you," Maggie jabbed her finger in the dead center of his chest, "at the scene of a crime."

John's eyes twitched. He pulled a cloth out of his pocket and nervously dusted a shelf loaded with t-shirts. I could see the tremble in his hand.

"John?" I kept my voice friendly. While she played bad cop, I'd try to reel him in with sugar. "Brent's boat is docked right next to Marcus. Did you know that?"

"Not until I got there. But Marcus wasn't there when I arrived," John added defensively. As soon as the words were out, he covered his mouth, realizing his mistake.

Maggie's face split into a big grin. "Marcus wasn't there. How convenient." She kept tapping that box of matches as if waiting for it to spontaneously combust for a shocking dramatic effect. "Who planned the fire, you or Brent?"

"We. Didn't. Do. It," he said through clenched teeth. "We were sitting in Brent's boat minding our own business, moaning about what a disaster the weekend was turning into. It was worse for Brent than me for obvious reasons, but still bad. Then suddenly, we heard people running down the dock. We rushed outside and saw the smoke."

Maybe it went down the way John said it had. Or, maybe John and Brent were covering for each other.

Someone set that fire as a warning to Marcus, but who?

29

*O*nce Maggie and I were out on the sidewalk, I confided my feelings about John and his story. "John seemed nervous, don't you think? Especially when he talked about being at the marina when Marcus's boat was on fire."

Maggie bobbed her head in agreement. "Oh, yes. Very suspicious. Ten to one he's hiding something. But what bothers me more is why Brent didn't tell me he was on the boat with Larry. If he's not going to be honest with me, how can I help him?"

"Let's go to the marina and have a look around," I suggested. "It's a great day for a walk."

"Now you're talking." She picked up her stride.

"If we don't find Brent there, maybe Kyle will provide us with more details."

As we walked, Pip pranced ahead of us like she was a celebrity. It made me wonder about her life before she was found almost starved to death on the beach after a terrible storm. She was so well behaved, I had to assume she'd belonged to someone who doted on her.

"So, Dani," Maggie said pulling me out of my daydreams about Pip's unknown couple of years. "What have you got planned for my birthday?"

"Ha! Nice try, Mags. I said I'd surprise you so don't expect any details. You'll find out after I pick you up tomorrow night. Six o'clock sharp and that's all I'm saying." I ran my thumb and finger over my lips, turned them, and threw away the imaginary key.

"Oh, come on," she said, pouting. "I hate surprises. Just give me a teensy clue, and I'll guess. All you have to do is nod yes or shake your head no. That way you won't actually give anything away."

I shook my head, pointing to my sealed lips.

"Oh, come on, Dani. What if I hate the surprise? Then you'll feel like a piece of slimy seaweed on the beach that Pip rolled in."

I laughed out loud.

"Those lips came unsealed, so give me a clue." She sounded much too confident.

"No way. Give a private investigator a teensy clue? You'd have the whole night figured out before we get to the marina." This job was proving to be more difficult than I'd anticipated. Maggie wasn't one to take no for an answer.

"Well, tell me what to wear, at least. I don't want to walk into a fancy schmancy nightclub with my comfy jeans and t-shirt on when every other woman is wearing a short, slinky dress."

The satisfied look on her face told me she thought she had me in a corner.

"Do you want to go to a fancy nightclub?" Answering a question with a question would buy me some time.

"Not really."

"Good. If you wear something comfortable without holes or stains, you'll be fine."

When we arrived at the marina, I unhooked Pip's leash, and she wasted no time darting to the tall grass at the edge of the parking lot. A different, newer boat bobbed in the slip once belonging to Wilhelmina.

"That must be Brent's boat," I said to Maggie. "Let's see if he's there."

She stopped me. "You wait here. I work for him, and I want a few words with him alone. Maybe you can find Kyle. I'd imagine this has been a nightmare for him as the marina manager."

That was perfectly fine with me. Avoiding Brent's boat meant there was less chance of running into Marcus. He was the last person I wanted to talk to at the moment. I wouldn't put it past him to find some way to make it look like I'd started the fire even though I was miles away.

I wandered toward Pip, glad to see Kyle down on one knee, laughing, and giving her hugs while she licked his face. It made me wonder if I'd made the right choice bringing Misty to Alice's home. At that moment, when I first found her, when Misty was lost and heartbroken, it seemed to be the best decision.

"Kyle," I said as I got closer so I wouldn't startle him, "she's got your number."

"I'm thinking about getting a dog," he said. He must have noticed my worried expression, because he quickly filled in with, "Don't worry, I don't mean reclaiming Misty. She's in the right place for her. I want to give some poor dog that's been cooped up at a shelter a new lease on life. A younger dog that needs this fresh air and freedom and likes people."

"There are plenty out there waiting for you," I said, relieved to hear his news.

"I know. When I went to the shelter looking for Misty, one in particular caught my attention, and I've decided he's the one for me. He's kind of goofy with one ear that sticks up and one down and his tongue is always hanging out on one side. His name is Duncan."

"That's fantastic, Kyle. Duncan will be one of the lucky ones to get a great forever home."

"I think *I'm* the lucky one, and I haven't even gotten him yet." He stood up. "Can you tell I'm excited? Anyway, what can I do for you today, Dani?"

"I'm here with Maggie. She needed to talk to her client, Brent. Turns out he never told her that he was on his boat with John Harmon when the fire started on Marcus's boat."

"Brent didn't start the fire," Kyle said. "He and John came out of his boat after Marcus and I saw the smoke."

"I'm not saying either one started it, but they were there, and could have done it, and that's what Maggie wants to discuss with him. We just talked to John and he acted guilty even if he's not." I shrugged as if I didn't care much either way. "Any idea how it started?"

"Wish I did. When I saw the smoke, my first thought was that the whole marina might go up in flames. Marcus was lucky that I grabbed a big fire extinguisher and put it out before it did much damage. Funny thing is, the fire was in his little stainless steel sink. It hadn't flamed up enough to catch onto anything else."

"What was burning?" I asked.

"It looked like some papers, maybe boat advertisements or something like that. I didn't take the time to get a close look at that detail, and by the time I doused it, there wasn't anything recognizable left. Or maybe I just have boats on my mind with talk of expanding the marina and people wanting to get bigger boats. Everything seems to be happening all at once."

"I guess he was lucky then. I suppose he'll be blogging about it."

"I asked him not to, but I doubt he'll listen to me. I don't want the marina to get any negative publicity."

"You got Wilhelmina's boat moved out of the way quickly to make room for Brent's boat."

"At least we have a paying customer in that spot now."

"Was Larry around last night when the fire started?"

"As a matter of fact, he was. He said he was checking his boat, that he had a funny feeling something odd was going to happen."

Why did Larry pretend to be surprised when I told him about the fire if he was there?

How interesting that the three people with the most to gain from Wilhelmina's murder—Brent, Larry, and John—were at the marina when the fire started.

But who killed Wilhelmina, ambushed Lily, and tried to burn Marcus's boat?

Was it *one* of them or were they working together?

30

*M*aggie waved to me from the back of Brent's boat, gesturing enthusiastically for me to hop onto it and join her.

What now?

"Come on, Pip. Maggie's about to lose it. Maybe Brent told her something important."

Pip, no slacker when it came to boats, dashed down the dock and jumped on next to Maggie. I wasn't far behind with my growing curiosity spurring me along.

Maggie reached across the small gap between the dock and the boat, grabbing my hand and pulling me over. "Brent says he heard noises on Marcus's boat last night before the fire started."

"Did he see anyone?"

"No. He said he was too busy making a sales pitch to sell his boat to John. They both jumped when they heard a thump and then Larry poked his head through the cabin door."

"*After* he heard the other noises?"

"Right. He doesn't know if it means anything but—"

"It puts all three of them right here where the action was."

"Exactly."

"Brent, Larry, and John never seem to be far from the action. What now?" I asked tilting my head and glancing around Maggie to see if Brent was near his cabin door. Although I didn't know what difference it would make. He was the one who told all this to Maggie in the first place.

He had his back to us, talking on his phone and gesturing with his free hand.

"Mags?" I kept my voice very low and calm. "Brent's on his phone. Do you think there's any chance he's calling for help to, I don't know, take care of us if we're getting too close to the killer or killers?"

"Let's not wait to find out." Maggie jumped off the boat. "Let's get out of here. He's not giving me any more information, anyway."

We hightailed it off the dock. Why had we walked to the marina? Right now, I'd feel so much safer tucked inside a car speeding back to town instead of being out in the open close to traffic.

Maggie yelled at me over her shoulder. "What are you doing?"

"I'm clipping Pip's leash on so she doesn't get distracted chasing after birds or squirrels. There. All set." I jogged to catch up.

"I'm not sure what to do." Maggie said. "On the one hand, AJ hates it if I interfere in his investigation, but he should know that all three of those men were on Brent's boat around the time of the fire."

"I'll tell him. That way he can get mad at me instead of you."

"You'll do that?"

"Sure. Now let's get back to town."

A dark car with tinted windows swerved as we jogged along the edge of the blacktop. Road rubble hit my legs like little needle pricks, dust swirled in my eyes, and a swoosh of air blew my curls to one side. The car was way too close for comfort.

"What the?" I didn't even finish my thought as I dusted myself off and tried to get a good look at the license plate, but the car had already disappeared around a bend in the road.

"Maggie? Do you think that car was trying to hit us?" My heart pounded harder than a jackhammer.

"Nope. If that was the intent, we'd be lying bloodied on the side of the road now. It came close enough to give us a big scare, though."

I raked my fingers through my hair to get it back into some kind of order and out of my face. "Did you get a good look with those x-ray eyes of yours?" I hoped she noticed something to identify the out of control driver.

"I couldn't see the driver, but the license plate started with an *L* and the car had a long scrape on the passenger side."

"We are walking on the wrong side of the road. Maybe the driver just didn't see us until the last second," I said. At least that's what I preferred to think. If someone intentionally tried to hit us or scare us, that was more than I wanted to believe.

"Yeah, maybe," Maggie said, but her tone and eye roll indicated she thought I was out of my mind.

Once we were back on the sidewalk, we slowed down to catch our breath. "Let's check on Lily and Rose, but don't tell them we almost got sideswiped since we don't have any details and it will only make them worry," I said.

"Okay. For now. But don't fool yourself, Dani. I'm inclined to think that car swerved at us intentionally. And, if that's the case, we can probably narrow the owner to one of three people."

I didn't like where this conversation was headed. "Brent, Larry, or John?"

"That's right."

"But you're working for Brent," I said, expressing disbelief that he could have done something so despicable.

Maggie stopped and turned me to face her. "Listen to me, Dani. I don't think Brent killed Wilhelmina, but there's always a small chance that I'm wrong. He could be innocent or a really good liar. After all, she was trying to destroy his business. There's nothing to put him near Sea Breeze when Lily got ambushed, but he *was* near Marcus's boat. You have to be careful around all of them."

"And John? He would have been at his store."

"Even John," Maggie insisted. "Maybe he stepped out for a minute. But most of all, Larry. That marina expansion could be a life saver for his business."

I grabbed Maggie's arm. "I just remembered that Chad told me he heard that Larry has a new business model for next spring—bigger and better. And,

Kyle said the papers that were burning on Marcus's boat looked like boat advertisements. Maybe Larry used some ads to start the fire."

"Does Kyle have those papers?"

"No. He said by the time he put the fire out, the papers were a pile of ashes. He must have just gotten a quick glimpse when he first got to the fire."

"Do you think Kyle or his father could have killed Wilhelmina?" Maggie asked.

"Kyle said he was the only relative who liked her. He's been very open and friendly toward me. As far as his father is concerned, I don't think he's around much. Kyle runs the marina, but any final decision has to go through his father. As far as I know, I've never even seen him in town. Have you?"

"No, I don't know what he looks like so I wouldn't know him if I saw him. Besides, it doesn't mean he couldn't have been here the night Wilhelmina was murdered while the whole town was fast asleep."

"Then the attack on Lily and the fire on Marcus's boat aren't related to the murder? Or, are you saying he managed to sneak in and out of town several times, commit a crime, and leave unnoticed? Once, *maybe*, but three times?"

"Yeah, you're right. Not a likely scenario."

I didn't see the dark green MG next to the Blue-berry Bay Grapevine, but we climbed the stairs to Maggie's apartment anyway.

"Anyone here?" she called after she opened the door.

Only a pathetic mew met our ears. Radar climbed right up Maggie's pants leg like it was a tree.

"Good thing I've got jeans on with those needle claws." She gently pried Radar off her pants and cuddled her under her chin. "Where did your guests go?"

I zeroed in on a piece of paper tucked under a mug—Rose's traditional old-fashioned habit.

"*Gone to Sea Breeze with Lily*," I read. "I suppose that makes sense. They can enjoy the ocean instead of listening to the traffic here on Main Street."

"What's wrong with the traffic noise?" Maggie asked with a fake hurt look on her face. "You'd rather hear the musical crash of ocean waves?"

"And the seagulls," I added. "Don't forget, I lived here for a year, so I know what I'm missing."

Maggie tucked Radar into a blanket and stuffed it into a shallow tote. "Let's take her to the ocean. She hasn't experienced the good life yet."

"Okay, but don't forget about Trouble. He's not going to be happy."

"Oh," Maggie flicked her wrist dismissively, "maybe he'll surprise you."

Right, I thought. There was a reason that cat was named Trouble. Plus, as far as all the recent surprises were concerned, I would much prefer to live without them. Every one.

But who was behind them? That's what I wanted to know.

31

I had to ride shotgun in Maggie's Ford Explorer to Sea Breeze since Rose had driven the MG.

I couldn't complain. It was *her* car that she let me use almost one hundred percent of the time.

Maggie pulled the back door open and said, "Hop in, Pipsqueak. Dani's riding up front with the important job of holding Radar's tote bag and keeping that curious kitten out of mischief."

Pip jumped in, but I could tell by the way she paced back and forth that she wasn't thrilled with having her seat downgraded. She was used to being the cool co-pilot. She did settle down, most likely happy to have any ride instead of being left behind.

It only took me a minute to discover what

Maggie meant about keeping her kitten under control. Without some kind of extra restraint, Radar would have crawled all over the Explorer. She kept my hands busy as I tried to confine the fur ball to the bag on my lap.

"Have you traveled with her before?" I asked Maggie, thinking I needed at least one more pair of hands and two more would have been even better.

She laughed as she quickly looked over at the big green eyes staring at her and the pathetic mewling begging for freedom. "Only when I brought her home from the police station, but she was so tiny then, she couldn't climb out of the box. I'll have to get a travel kennel. I can't imagine she'll ever sit quietly and look out the window like Pip does."

"Are cats even meant to ride in cars?" I managed to catch the escape artist at the last second before she made it all the way out of the tote bag. "I suspect she'd be sitting on your shoulder or head or maybe on the steering wheel if you were traveling alone. She's more than a handful." Radar managed to squirm out of my hands and climb to my shoulder, but I gently pried her sharp claws free from my shirt before she took a flying leap to the back seat. This one was fearless.

Pip's wet nose on my cheek let me know someone was feeling neglected.

"Jealous, are you?" I asked. But I didn't dare let go of Radar with one hand to give Pip a reassuring pat. "We're almost there." What I didn't say out loud was that now Pip would have the kitten *and* the ornery one-eyed cat to deal with. Poor Pip.

When Maggie turned between the two stones that marked the entrance to Sea Breeze, a loud, "What's going on here?" fell out of my mouth.

In addition to the dark green MG, Sue Ellen's red Escalade, Luke's truck, and AJ's black Jeep were all lined up behind Rose's Cadillac.

"If AJ brought his kitty, the two could play together," Maggie said.

Was she serious? I didn't share her enthusiasm.

But judging by the grin on her face, Maggie was dead serious.

"There's a murderer to find before he manages to wreak more mayhem in Misty Harbor," I said. The sooner this crime was solved and behind me, the better. Yes, the pressure of everything weighed heavily on me.

"As cute as these fur balls are, this is no time to have kittens playing tag on the back of Rose's couch or hide and seek underneath."

As we walked past the cars to the house, AJ came out, surprised to see us. "Oh, there you are, Maggie. I stopped by your apartment earlier with a bit of a problem I needed help with, but Rose has it all under control."

The sheepish grin on his face gave him away. He couldn't fool me; he had her surprise birthday party in mind. How would he explain this new problem when Maggie pried? That would be interesting.

"What kind of problem?" she asked.

"It's Leo. He managed to get himself stuck at the top of my highest bookshelf, and I didn't want to leave him home alone until I could figure out a remedy for the problem. I thought maybe you'd be able to keep him with you and Radar until I got my house kitten-proofed."

"Leo?" I looked between AJ and Maggie.

"Leo the Lion," AJ said with over-sized pride. "Clever, right? Wait till you see him, Dani."

Maggie looked at me with a don't-believe-the-exaggerations eye roll.

I still wasn't convinced this wasn't just a made-up problem on AJ's part so it didn't look suspicious that he was here consulting about the party. At any rate, it was what it was, and now Pip would have to contend with Leo, Radar *and* Trouble ganging up on her.

"Happy to help, AJ. Maybe Radar can teach Leo how to climb up *and* down. *She* never needs help from me." Maggie spoke with obvious glee in her voice that *her* kitten had superior intelligence and well-developed climbing skills. Apparently, competition between these two extended above and beyond mere crime fighting to include which kitten had better agility.

"AJ?" I said, hoping to jog them away from their kitten obsession and back to the matter that had taken over our town. "Someone tried to run us over earlier."

His eyes darkened into narrow slits. "Are you sure? Let's go inside. You can tell me everything."

I carried the tote with Radar into the house behind Pip and Maggie. AJ followed last.

It only took a couple of minutes for Radar to find her sibling and lead him off to who knew where. If they got into trouble, we'd hear their pitiful cries for help.

Pip looked at me as if to say, I'm too mature for that stuff.

Trouble was busy napping on Rose's lap or else just ignoring the invasion.

We settled down in the living room where Maggie, sitting straight and tall, recounted every detail about our close call after we left the marina on foot.

"A dark sedan with tinted windows, traveling into Misty Harbor at approximately forty miles an hour, swerved right at us when we were minding our own business walking from the marina on the edge of the road," she said without stopping to take a breath.

"I got a quick glimpse of the license plate, which contained the letter *L*, and saw a long scrape on the passenger side of the car," she added.

AJ jotted in his notebook as Maggie detailed the incident. "Anything else? Like, why did you walk to the marina in the first place?"

"The decision to walk was to get some exercise. Our destination to the marina was simple—John at Hidden Treasures told us he'd been there with Brent the night before. I had to talk to Brent. My client."

"Oh?" AJ leaned forward. Obviously, this tidbit of information caught him by surprise.

"For some reason," I said, "John was under the impression that Brent wouldn't share that detail." I shrugged at how ridiculous that sounded. "What was he thinking to believe Brent would take all the suspicion on himself when he could spread it around?"

Maggie added another detail. "Brent said they heard some noise coming from Marcus's boat, and then Larry poked his head into Brent's cabin."

AJ scanned through a few pages of his notes. "So, Brent, John, *and* Larry were all at the marina last night. I have to assume it was before the fire because Kyle told me he saw Brent and John when he and Marcus saw the smoke on Marcus's boat. Kyle never mentioned Larry being there, though."

"Well," I said. "Kyle told me that Larry was at the marina checking on his boat because he had a funny feeling that something might happen. He didn't tell me that he ever saw Larry on Brent's boat, either. That bit of information came from Brent."

AJ snapped his notebook closed. "So much for enjoying the company of all you beautiful ladies, but I'm heading to the marina for another chat with Kyle."

"Oh, another thing Kyle told me," I said to AJ, deciding to lay all my cards on the table with the hope that he would share something important, too.

"He said the fire on Marcus's boat looked like it was started with boat advertisements."

"Yeah, he did tell me that detail." AJ stood up.

"I'll follow you out, AJ. With my hands full keeping Radar in her tote, I forgot my bag in Maggie's car." Pip must have heard the word out and decided she could use a break from too many kitties. This was the perfect excuse for both of us to walk out and let me talk to AJ without everyone else butting in on our conversation. I wanted his opinion about who I should worry about the most. At the same time, Pip could get a breath of fresh cat-free air.

Once we were alone outside, I said, "Chad, one of my new employees, is friends with Brent."

AJ waited for me to catch up to him.

"Chad told me a couple of interesting things about Larry."

"I'm listening."

We both stood next to AJ's Jeep with the scent of salty air drifting around us from the cool ocean breeze. I pulled my fleece tight.

"The night that Brent met up with Wilhelmina, she told him she wanted to put both Brent and Larry out of business." I paused to let that information sink in. "He didn't say why, but my guess is that she thought they were the biggest contributors to the single-use trash problem."

"You think that one of them decided to get Wilhelmina out of their life? For good?"

I nodded, glad that AJ came to a similar conclusion as mine. "I think things are pointing toward Larry. He has also been heard bragging about having a bigger and better business plan for next spring. Getting the Best Business Award is his first step toward this new goal."

"Let me get this straight." AJ held up a finger. "You think that Larry killed Wilhelmina to end the protests." Another finger popped up. "He ambushed Lily as a warning for you to stop asking so many questions." A third finger joined the others. "Then, he tried to burn down Marcus's boat?" Four fingers now waved in front of my face. "Oh, and if that wasn't enough, he tried to run you over. But why target Marcus's boat? What does *he* have to do with all this?"

"Maybe to make him stop with all his negative blogging about Misty Harbor. Larry depends on the tourists more than the rest of us."

"That's an interesting theory, but I need facts." AJ dropped his hand and walked to Maggie's Explorer with me following. "Do you think I'll be able to squeeze out of here? I'd hate to go inside and ask everyone to move their cars."

I paced off the space between Maggie's Explorer and the stone marker. "You should be able to get by." A mark on the white stone caught my attention. I traced my finger along the long black streak.

"What is that?" AJ asked.

"Paint from a dark car?" As soon as the words left my mouth, the paint connected the dots. "From a careless driver that ambushed Lily and tried to hit Maggie and me today?" Icy fingers of fear ran up my spine.

Who owned the dark car that now sported a big scrape on the passenger side?

32

From where I stood in the driveway at Sea Breeze, I watched AJ's Jeep disappear around the corner. I heard a text message ting when I pulled my bag off the seat of Maggie's vehicle. After digging my phone out, I read the text from Chad and groaned. "Well, Pip, Chad says we need to go to the diner. Ready?"

Of course, at the word ready Pip, went on high alert. With an excited yip and tapping of her front paws in reply to my question, she let me know that she'd be at my side once I got moving.

I reached down and scratched under her ear. "You're the best, Pipsqueak."

I looked toward the house and decided against

going back inside. I'd just hear moaning about leaving so soon after just arriving. Instead, I sent a text to Luke explaining that Chad needed me at the diner.

Okay, I admit it. I took the cowardly way out.

I easily maneuvered the MG out of its spot behind the Cadillac, carefully backed out between the two rock markers, and turned the car toward town.

Pip, with a sparkle in her deep brown eyes, let me know she was happy to be up front in the co-pilot seat instead of restricted to the back. She took her favorite stance with her front paws on the dash, her *Best Dog* bandana billowing in the breeze from the half-opened window and gave two quick satis-fied barks.

I laughed at her enthusiasm. It was a tonic from all the problems surrounding me and encourage-ment to keep searching for answers. Wherever it would lead us.

As I enjoyed the view of Blueberry Bay that peeked between trees, a twinge of guilt stabbed my chest for being an absent owner during the past couple of days. On the other hand, because of this new-found freedom from the diner, I'd learned something important — I wasn't indispensable and appreciation for my two hardworking reliable employees skyrocketed. They were worth their weight in gold. At least I had one thing going right in my life.

I zipped into the small driveway next to the Little Dog Diner, closed for the day now, and headed inside with Pip.

Christy was putting the finishing touches on the gleaming surfaces of each booth, so they'd be ready first thing in the morning. I heard the freezer door in the kitchen slam closed.

"Looking good in here," I said to Christy, knowing that praise for a job well done was always appreciated and all too often overlooked.

She straightened and, with her forearm, pushed some stray hairs away from her face. "Thanks, Dani. We're almost ready to head home."

Wondering why Chad asked me to come to the diner, I headed into the kitchen where I found him cleaning the grill.

"What can I help you with?" I asked, feeling like I should be the one telling him what to do instead of waiting for his update.

After wiping his hands on his apron, he dumped

it into the laundry bag. "Larry was here looking for you. He muttered something about checking to make sure you're all right. Any idea what that's about?"

"Only that someone tried to run Maggie and me over, so finding a dark sedan that may have a white scrape on the passenger side is high on my agenda."

"Larry drives a black Honda," Chad informed me. "The car hit something?"

"It could be two different cars, but my gut is telling me that the car that left black paint when it sideswiped the rocks at Sea Breeze and the car that almost hit me are one and the same."

I shrugged as if this was a no brainer. "It's hard to imagine any other explanation."

"Maybe that's why Larry looked so worried when he came here looking for you. But I wonder why he didn't stop when it happened."

"If he was driving the car, maybe he came to his senses and decided he'd better fess up before Detective Crenshaw came looking for him."

"If you want to ask him, he said he'd be at Hidden Treasures with John Harmon discussing something about the Best Business Award." Chad busied himself sweeping the floor around the work area while we talked.

"Thanks for the heads up. I promise I'll be around to help as soon as this nasty murder business is wrapped up. Something new pops up like a bad nightmare whenever I turn around."

Chad leaned on his broom. "No worries, Christy and I have everything under control here. I prepped all the veggies for salads, sliced cheese and cold cuts for sandwiches, made up a list of items we're running low on, and took out frozen soups to thaw overnight. I'm happy to come in extra early tomorrow to bake a variety of muffins and the ever-popular streusel coffee cake to refill the display. You can totally count on us." He raised his eyebrows waiting for my reply.

"You don't know how much that means to me to have two hard-working reliable people here." My emotions jumped from fearful to thankful, leaving me feeling weepy. I pulled myself together, though, and said, "Thanks for filling in for me. You and Christy are doing a great job here."

Chad clipped the broom back on its wall bracket. "It works both ways. We love this diner, the customers, and it's like a dream come true that we can work together at a job we love." He waved both hands shooing me out. "Go find Larry and maybe you'll solve one or two of your mysteries."

I opened my mouth to say I'd stay and close up the diner but decided it was in good hands, and he wouldn't let me do it anyway.

"Dani?"

I turned around.

"Be careful, okay?"

"I've got Pip with me so don't worry about a thing." I smiled at Chad to reinforce a brave image, even though I felt a few trembles inside.

"Pip, let's go."

She danced around my legs, not waiting to be asked twice. With Pip at my side, any worry about confronting Larry was just a fleeting nag. Besides, I told myself as I walked to the door, talking at Hidden Treasures kept us in plain sight with customers milling around. In addition, my adrenalin surge would keep my observation skills on high alert.

Of course, as Pip and I walked along Main Street, most people either smiled or asked me about my sidekick, which slowed our progress to a crawl. Pip loved the attention, but I kept us moving toward our destination.

A bell jingled when I pulled the Hidden Treasures door open. Was it my imagination, or did the bell sound like shattering glass?

"Be more careful!" a woman's voice hissed at a young boy as she pulled him and pushed me out of the way. "Let's get out of here before I have to pay for that worthless souvenir."

As I moved farther into the store, my shoe crunched, and the noise I'd heard now made sense. "Oh, Pippy, be careful." I scooped her into my arms seconds before she stepped on the sharp pieces of glass.

"Dani?" John approached from the rear of the store. "Did your dog knock something over?"

"No. Your customer just streaked out of here before you could charge her for the broken item."

John's lips pulled together as if he thought I was guilty of the accident and blaming someone else. "Today has been going like that. I'll get a broom. If you're here to talk to Larry, he's in the back. He was hoping you'd come."

"What's going on?"

"He needs to talk to you." John left me standing in the broken glass while he disappeared to get a broom.

I inhaled deeply to calm my nerves. Pip and I crunched toward the back of the store where it was deserted of customers. I felt uncomfortable at best.

Pip wiggled in my arms, but I didn't dare let her down.

We found Larry sitting in a chair with his head in his hands.

I stood frozen in place, afraid to move closer.

"Larry? What's going on?"

33

"*L*arry?" I repeated barely above a whisper. "You wanted to talk to me?" I glanced behind me wondering if I should just turn around and run for the exit.

Finally, he lifted his head. "You're alright?" As he looked at me, relief flooded his face. "I'm sorry I didn't stop."

"It *was* you that almost hit us?"

"I didn't even see you until the last second when I swerved away. You were in the shadows. On the wrong side of the road. I don't know why I didn't stop then but I guess I was too focused on my meeting with Marcus. Once the scene replayed in my head, I realized it was you with your dog."

"And Maggie," I added.

"As soon as it all hit me, I went to the Little Dog Diner to apologize, but you weren't there. Chad didn't know where you were or if you were even okay. I'm so sorry, Dani. I've been a mess wondering if I'd let my obsession over my business make me lose sight of more important things."

I set Pip down but pulled her close with the leash. She sniffed Larry's shoes. Larry reached down to scratch under her ear, which was a sure way to make friends with her. I wasn't sure I approved.

"Can I ask you a question, Larry?"

"Sure." He continued the scratching. Pip jumped into his lap to make it easier.

"Did you go to Sea Breeze Friday night?"

His whole body tensed. He sucked in a breath of air. "I did. I was pretty angry Friday night about AJ postponing the Best Business Award and I went to talk to Rose because I thought she was behind the decision. Honestly? I thought she was trying to give you an advantage. But, while I sat in my car, I came to my senses and admitted to myself that you deserve the award and I was only being petty, so I left."

That had to be a difficult admission from Larry. "Did you pull into the driveway?"

"Yeah."

"Do you remember if you scraped one of the stone markers on your way out?"

"Huh. I didn't know where I got that scrape, but it's possible."

Was he lying? "Lily was ambushed in the driveway."

"What? No one was in the driveway when I pulled in, only Sue Ellen's car."

"Someone attacked her, and you just said you were there." Pip jumped off Larry's lap and sniffed as far as her leash let her explore.

His mouth fell open. "Oh, my word. Is she okay?"

"She suffered a concussion, but she'll be fine."

"Listen, Dani. I never got out of my car and when I left, a car sped by so fast, I took the turn out of your driveway a little too tight. I guess I could have scraped that rock without realizing it. If there's any damage, I'll pay to fix it."

"It's a *rock*, Larry." I said hearing frustration in my tone. "The rock is fine. The question is, if you were there but didn't get out and attack Lily," a big if in my mind, "who did?"

"I don't know. Honestly, I didn't see anyone."

I wasn't going to argue with him about this. The

truth would come out at some point. "So, you said you were so focused on your meeting with Marcus that you didn't stop after you nearly killed me. It must have been an earth-shattering meeting," I said with sarcasm dripping like hot fat.

"It was about his blog. He told me if I didn't talk to him and give my side of events surrounding Wilhelmina's murder, he'd write something I'd regret." Larry ran his fingers through his thinning hair. "Listen, Dani, I can't afford any negative articles about my touring business. As it is, I'm hanging on by the skin of my teeth in the hope that the marina expands so I can get a bigger tour boat."

"About that," I said. "Wilhelmina's murder certainly benefits you if the marina does expand."

His eyes flashed as he understood my implication.

"For crying out loud, Dani. *I* didn't kill Wilhelmina. You can ask Kyle. I was trying to work with her on a solution to the litter problem. As annoying as she was, she brought attention to a real issue, and I want Blueberry Bay sparkling clean as much as anyone else."

I had to admit that what he said made sense. "Were you getting anywhere with her?"

"Unfortunately, no."

The sound of footsteps made me turn as John joined us.

"Okay," he said. "I locked the door. Today has been nothing but people breaking stuff or wanting gossip about the murder and not about buying... a completely wasted day," he complained, as if this day couldn't end soon enough for him. "Wasted weekend."

Great. Here I was, locked inside Hidden Treasures with John Harmon and Larry Sidwell, two suspects in Wilhelmina Joy's murder. I didn't want them to see my fear and to know I suspected them. Just in case.

"Larry, you mentioned Kyle earlier. Do you think he might have murdered Wilhelmina to get her out of the way so the marina expansion could move forward?"

"I've wondered the same thing," he answered.

Interesting. "Kyle told me he was fond of his Aunt Willy." I angled myself so I had a clear path to the door.

"Ha! He may have told you that, but Kyle knows how to play the friendly laid-back guy in any situation. He's learned from the best... his father. I witnessed plenty of arguments Kyle had with his

Aunt Willy when he was trying to get her to pay her bills. She just laughed in his face."

John nodded in agreement. "Kyle's the kind of person who will smile right in your face, but when you turn around, watch out."

I hadn't noticed any of that when I was around Kyle. From what I'd observed, he was kind, calm, and competent. Had I missed something? "Larry, did you have that meeting with Marcus about his blog?"

"Sort of. I know that sounds like a ridiculous answer. The thing is, when we met, all he did was talk about himself and how his blog was going to shock everyone. Right, John?"

John nodded in agreement. "I hope he was just spouting a lot of nothing with all his bragging about this next blog post. Otherwise, he might be making life more miserable for all of us. You too, Dani. He said that his opinion is that none of us deserve any award."

"Why? What's it to him?" I asked.

"It's his way to make himself feel important," Larry said.

"And get his followers all ramped up for whatever he writes," John added.

"I can't be bothered with that right now," I said,

getting fed up with this conversation. "The fact is, someone murdered Wilhelmina, and he's out there still. Probably laughing at all of us while we get jumpier and jumpier."

Larry held his hands up. "Slow down a minute. How do you know it's a he and not a she?"

"When Lily got ambushed, a male voice said, 'your friend is trouble.' I'm assuming that Wilhelmina's murder, Lily's ambush, and the fire on Marcus's boat are all related."

I looked from Larry to John to gage their reaction. From the looks on their faces, I didn't think they were hiding anything. "So," I continued, "if neither of you were involved in any of that, it leaves Brent."

"Or Kyle," Larry quickly added.

"Let's talk about Brent first," I said. "Wilhelmina was murdered in his café, which was in financial trouble. He wanted her slip at the marina for *his* boat. He was next to Marcus's boat when the fire started. He could have been at Sea Breeze and ambushed Lily."

I paused thinking about all these incidents from murder to assault to arson.

"John, by any chance do you remember if Brent

ever came in here to buy those little plastic lobsters you sell?"

"As a matter of fact, he bought a couple dozen last Thursday. He said he would give them out to kids that came into the café for the Best of Blueberry Bay Weekend. Why?"

"Lily found one after she was ambushed."

Both Larry and John's mouths dropped open. They looked genuinely shocked at that revelation.

This was something for AJ to sort out.

I liked Brent and hated to think he was behind any of the recent dark events. But desperation could be a powerful motivation. And if I had learned anything, Brent was desperate to keep his café profitable.

I had to get all this solved before Misty Harbor suffered another dreadful incident.

My most important question now? Was I still in danger?

34

*I*t was obvious from Pip's prancing that she wanted to leave Hidden Treasures as much as I did. Before I left, I promised to keep Larry and John informed of anything I learned.

Once back on the sidewalk my jaw fell open when I saw AJ heading straight for me. Or, was his destination Hidden Treasures? I couldn't tell until he stopped in front of me.

"Dani? I thought you were still at Sea Breeze. What brought you back into town?"

Pip jumped on AJ's legs demanding attention, and he obliged with a quick scratch on her belly.

"I needed to see Chad at the diner."

AJ looked up at the Hidden Treasures sign hanging above us. "Are you lost?"

"No. Chad told me that Larry needed to see me, so," I shrugged innocently. "Larry and John were here discussing—"

He finished my sentence. "An alibi?"

"An alibi for what?" Hmmm, I wondered. Had AJ uncovered some important information? Why else would he be heading to Hidden Treasures? He bumped into me by accident.

"I've identified the car that almost ran you over and hit that rock at Sea Breeze. It belonged to Larry Sidwell. What did he tell you? That someone stole his car?"

I shook my head. "No, not at all. He admitted to it all, but he didn't try to run us down intentionally. Maggie and I were walking on the wrong side of the road in a shadow, and he said that he didn't see me."

"And the scrape on his car? How'd he weasel his way out of that?" It was obvious that AJ wasn't going to be easily taken in by excuses from Larry. Was I too gullible?

"He said he did go to Sea Breeze but never got out of his car. He scraped the rock when another car drove by too fast, and on his way out of the drive-way, he cut the corner too close." Now that I relayed the excuse, it sounded much weaker than when Larry spun it for me.

"And you believe all that?"

Did I?

"Did Larry also tell you that he left the marina at about the same time Wilhelmina left on the night she met Brent at his café." He leaned close to me. "The night she was murdered?"

"No," I answered, dragging out the word. "How did you find this out?"

"I just had a long chat with Kyle."

"Kyle told me that he saw Wilhelmina leave with her sign on her way to Brent's café. He regretted that he didn't stop her. Doesn't it sound suspicious that today he added in a new detail about Larry?"

"What?"

"Did you listen to what I just said? Kyle knew where Wilhelmina was going, and she had her sign. *Now* he's telling you that he saw Larry leave at the same time? Why didn't he tell me that important detail when he talked to me about all this yesterday? Why now? It sounds like he's trying to deflect attention from himself."

"Maybe." AJ went quiet for a moment, taking in all that I said.

"And, what about Kyle's relationship with his Aunt Willy," I continued. "Isn't that what he affectionately called her? I heard that they had plenty of arguments over her lack of paying for her marina slip which, in my opinion, wouldn't make for the affectionate relationship he pretended they had."

I took a deep breath and forced myself to calm down. I wanted to sound clear-headed and believable, not hysterical. "There's one more thing I just learned, AJ."

"I can't wait," he said sarcastically.

"Lily found a plastic lobster on the seat of Sue Ellen's car after she got ambushed."

He dismissed my comment with a wave of his hand. "With Sue Ellen's obsession with anything red, it doesn't surprise me that she'd have a little souvenir like that."

"You might find this shocking, but it wasn't Sue Ellen's souvenir." I took another deep breath and waited for his undivided attention. "It turns out, Brent bought a couple dozen of the little plastic lobster souvenirs on Thursday. I'd like to know what he says about that. Maybe you should have a chat with him."

AJ shook his head as if trying to clear cobwebs. "Brent has a lot on his plate, and this bit of information won't help him, that's for sure. It's crazy to think that a little piece of plastic could be an important clue in this mystery." AJ took a step closer to Hidden Treasures but kept his attention on me. "Where are you headed now?"

"I'm tired. Back to the diner to pick up the list Chad left for me, then home to Sea Breeze, put my feet up, and try to relax."

"Good. And tomorrow night is all set with Maggie?"

"*My* part is all set. As far as Maggie is concerned, you're about as popular as a big seagull dropping, if that's what you mean by 'all set.' I hope you know what you're doing, AJ. And, by the way, what's with this kitten competition you two have going?"

AJ laughed a deep belly laugh. "Isn't it great? She thinks Radar is somehow superior to Leo, and she refuses to admit that my kitty has softer fur and the cutest little meow."

"Oh, *please*. I can't *believe* you're talking like that, AJ."

"Right, and you *never* ooh and aah over the adorable Pipster?" He tilted his head and lifted both eyebrows letting me know he saw right through *my* own passion.

We both laughed, giving my nerves a much-needed release from all the recent tension. Yes, getting home and sitting on the patio at Sea Breeze was just what I needed.

AJ pulled Hidden Treasures' door open and said before he entered, "After my chat with Larry and John, I'll head to Brent's house and see what he says about those lobster souvenirs. From what Josie tells me, which isn't much, she says Brent is pretty depressed about the café and barely leaves the house. She swears he'd never kill anyone or trash his own business, but, of course, as his loyal spouse, I wouldn't expect her to say anything else."

AJ gave me a pat on my back, I suppose to reassure me that everything would work out in the end.

As Pip and I made our way to the diner, I thought about how my relationship with AJ had grown. I appreciated that we'd developed this honest way of communicating. It sometimes got testy, but we usually ended on a comfortable note. Maybe that was the magic in his relationship with Maggie. They'd each found someone who tested the other and pushed them out of their comfort zone.

I let Pip off her leash so she could sniff around before we got in the car while I made a quick trip into the diner. Christy had all the booths sparkling, the floor gleaming, and everything else neat and tidy.

I grabbed Chad's list from the work area in the kitchen and tucked it in my pocket. That could wait until Monday.

With the diner doors securely locked behind me, I headed to the MG.

"What now?" I said when I saw Marcus Willoby pacing near my car. I had a sinking feeling that my plan of heading home to relax had just hit a roadblock. Didn't this guy understand that I had no intention of doing an interview with him? He just wouldn't give up.

"I'm glad I found you, Dani." Marcus's voice came out all in one quick rush of words. "Wilhelmina's dog is wandering around the marina like she's a poor lost soul."

My heart fell to my toes. Misty gone from Alice's house? "How long ago did you see her?"

"Not too long. Kyle told me you rehomed her, and I thought you'd be the best person to search for her."

"Thank you, Marcus," I managed to say as I opened the MG's door for Pip. She wasted no time jumping in. I'm sure she sensed my concern even if she didn't understand the problem. Or, maybe she did. At any rate, she'd help me find Misty.

Images of that sweet dog hit by a car after *my* near miss left me shaky.

I had to find Misty before something bad happened to her.

35

I screeched into the Misty Marina parking lot and parked under the shade of a towering maple tree. Before I began searching all helter-skelter, I called Alice to let her know I was on the hunt for Misty.

"Oh, thank you, Danielle," she said over the phone. "I don't know how she escaped. I think the gate in the backyard broke. I'll have to get someone to replace the latch. Please call me as soon as you find her."

"Of course." I hung up and sent a text to Luke to let him know what had happened. *On my way to help*, he texted back.

Pip practically flew out of the MG when I

opened my door and stuck her nose to the ground like a proper detective.

Marcus pulled in next to me. "Good luck. I'd help but that dog never liked me too much, just like her owner."

Kyle came up to us and I nodded hello to both of them. I proceeded to follow Pip. With her nose, she would track Misty better than anyone else I could think of.

"Dani?"

Jeez Louise, I thought. Why couldn't all these people leave me in peace? "I don't have time to talk right now, Kyle. Pip and I are looking for Misty."

He didn't take my hint and matched my strides. "That's what I want to talk about. If Alice can't keep control of Misty, maybe it's the wrong place for her."

I stopped, put my hands on my hips, and glared at him. "You can't take that dog away *now*. Something completely unexpected happened, and you can be sure that I'll scour her backyard and make it completely secure when I bring Misty back."

He huffed and stalked back toward his office building, which suited me just fine. I didn't want him tagging along.

By now, I'd lost track of the direction Pip had

taken, so I followed what looked like a well-worn path that paralleled the shoreline. If Misty got frightened, she could be anywhere, but this path went into town. I made the assumption that it might be familiar to Misty.

The wind carried Pip's familiar yipping in my direction. I broke into a jog and veered off the trail into scrubby brush, slowing my pace to push branches aside.

I could hear Pip's yips getting louder as the going got slower. Thorny branches whipped across my face as I battled through the thick underbrush. I slipped and scraped my legs clambering over boulders but finally, pushing one last branch aside, I found Pip in a small clearing.

Alone.

With a collar twirling on a branch above her.

It made no sense.

A loud grunt behind me made goosebumps erupt on my arms. "Hello?" I tried to make my voice sound strong.

"If you hadn't taken off so fast," Kyle said, as he came into view, "I could have saved you all this trouble." He ducked under a branch, dusted himself off, and approached me.

I backed up, moving away from Kyle until I was

next to Pip. She'd stopped her barking now that she brought me to her quarry.

Kyle moved closer to me.

I shifted away again as if we were engaged in some sort of weird dance. "What trouble?" I asked.

"Misty. She's safe on Brent's boat. Right after you disappeared, Marcus saw her heading down the dock toward the slip where Aunt Willy used to dock her boat. She jumped right onto Brent's boat, so he shut her in the cabin." He looked around the small clearing. "How'd you end up here?"

I glanced at the collar. "Pip must have followed Misty's scent here."

"Is that her collar?" Kyle reached up and yanked the purple collar off the branch.

"It doesn't make sense. Someone must have hung it up there. Was it you Kyle?"

His face pinched into a confused expression. "Why would I do that?"

"To lead me out here... get me away from every-one... shut me up. Someone wants me to stop asking questions about your aunt."

Pip growled.

Kyle held his hands up. "You think *I* killed Aunt Willy and almost set my own marina on fire?"

"I don't know what to think. Someone hurt Lily after giving her a message that I was trouble. What am I *supposed* to think?"

Kyle's arms dangled at his sides. His voice softened. "Dani, I'm not here to hurt you. I want to find out what happened to Aunt Willy. I know I was kind of abrupt with you about Misty, but I'm trying to keep everyone happy, and I haven't had a lot of luck." He held his hand out. "How about we walk back to the marina and you can get Misty."

I wanted to believe him, but I also didn't plan to take any chances. If I stayed behind him with Pip, I'd feel the safest. "You go first. Pip and I will follow."

"Okay."

As we walked, I asked Kyle, "Who do you think had the most to gain from Wilhelmina's death?"

"It's hard to say. Different people gained differently. I mean, look at Brent, Wilhelmina had impacted his café enormously."

"But," I interrupted, "don't you think the damage was already done? He's struggling and may not survive even with her protest over."

"Good point."

By now, we were out of the thick brush and

back on the trail heading toward the marina. I relaxed, thinking that now we were out in the open and if I'd misjudged Kyle, he wouldn't do anything to me here.

"Aunt Willy was a constant annoyance to John at Hidden Treasures," he said.

"But I can't imagine that it was enough for John to murder her."

"That leaves Larry. For many reasons, I guess I should have started with him, but I like the guy. He attracts lots of interesting people to the marina, and I'm excited about his new business plans for next year."

"But those plans wouldn't happen if Wilhelmina was still alive, right?"

"Not as easily or quickly. I was working around her complaints. Sure, it's easier now."

"Which brings this whole conversation back to you, Kyle."

He stopped suddenly.

His eyes darkened.

Instinctively, I leaned away from him and held my arms up for protection.

"What about *you* Dani? *You* found Aunt Willy. What led *you* to the café so early Friday morning?

Are you harassing everyone else to protect your-self?" He stalked off leaving me alone with Pip.

Was that what everyone was saying? I killed Wilhelmina and was running around looking for evidence to point to anyone else?

This was all wrong.

I had no choice but to find the answers.

36

The last stretch of trail to the marina provided an amazing view of Blueberry Bay—the ocean, the beaches, the town I loved—that I couldn't dream of losing.

Disappointment filled every fiber of my body after I scanned the parking lot of the marina, and Luke's truck was not in sight.

"It's just you and me, Pip. Let's get Misty and let her know she's not all alone in this world." I sent Luke a text telling him to meet me at Alice's house because Misty had been found.

Pip charged down the dock straight to Brent's boat. More and more, I believed this incredible terrier understood me when I talked to her.

I followed but without as much spring in my step as my loyal partner.

As I got abreast of Marcus's boat, I noticed that his cabin door was open with a folder on the table. I glanced around, but I couldn't see him inside or anyone else for that matter.

The folder begged to be opened. Should I take a quick look?

An irresistible surge of curiosity pulled me onto his boat, hoping to find out if the folder contained any information about his blog. It would only take a minute. I convinced myself that it was better to know in advance what we'd be facing once he published his latest rabble-rousing blog entry.

I flipped the folder open, shocked to see *my* name, DANIELLE MACKENZIE, in large bold letters under the headline — KILLER.

What? Had he already spread some kind of smear campaign about me? What else could I make of this awful headline staring at me right after hearing Kyle's accusation? I scanned the page: *Will Dani get speared to death like the woman she murdered before she causes more mayhem in Misty Harbor?*

My blood ran ice cold, and I turned to flee only to find the boat's owner staring at me.

"Dani, what a surprise," Marcus said. He leaned against his cabin door, effectively blocking my exit.

"I came in hoping to find you," I lied. I hoped my voice didn't reveal the terror building inside me. I shook with fear. Only Luke, the police and I knew how Wilhelmina was murdered. Except for the killer himself.

"Misty is safe and I'll be returning her to Alice now," I said. How could Marcus know the cause of death?

"Oh? Did you find her collar, too? Could you reach it?" The twisted grin on his face only made my heart pound harder. He had to be the one behind everything—Wilhelmina, Lily, and Misty. The fire, too?

"I did. So," I stepped toward him and the exit, "I'll be on my way now." I had to get by this sick man. He had some master plan. I wanted no part in it; I knew that for sure.

"I think we both know that won't be happening, Dani. You found something interesting while you were trespassing on my boat, didn't you?"

"Like what, Marcus?" Somehow, I had to buy time until someone figured out where I was. I inched closer to the door hoping for a chance to run past him.

"Cute. I like you. It's such a shame that you decided to poke around where you weren't invited. Now," he raised his hands and shrugged, "you'll end up just like Wilhelmina."

"Whom you speared with her own sign? No one knew that detail except me and the police." I probably should have kept my mouth shut and tried to bluff my way past him. Too late. I blew that plan.

"Now, now, now, Danielle. Don't get so picky. I call it poetic justice. Wilhelmina carried that sign everywhere... right to her end." He leaned toward me. "She was about to go to the police about my marijuana habit. Somehow, she discovered I didn't really have a prescription for it. With all the other people I supplied, I had to stop her." He waved his arm in a big circle. "I love it here and *she* wasn't going to win that battle." His eyes turned into dark slits. "No matter what."

"So, you killed her." I couldn't believe what he was telling me.

"If you had just let nature take its course and didn't keep *pushing* all your theories, *Brent* would be locked up because of his ill-timed, but convenient for me, meeting with her. Everyone knew she was destroying his business. That gave him means, motive, and opportunity. Then it looked like Larry might take the fall or even Kyle or John. It's been entertaining following your moves while you managed to dig up so many suspects. But," he threw his hands in the air, "you've outlasted your useful-ness to me. I wonder who will get blamed for *your* mysterious disappearance. Or, once I publish this latest blog, maybe everyone will just say you got what you deserved."

I looked into his cold, dark eyes. Is that what a marijuana habit did? No, I think something more evil lived in his heart. But somehow, I had to outwit him. "No one will believe it. Especially Rose. She'll find you if it takes her last breath."

Marcus chuckled with obvious enjoyment. "Good. I can't wait for that last breath because I've coveted that paper of hers *forever*. Maybe I'll keep the Little Dog Diner going, too. This whole plan to rid me of Wilhelmina is opening up a ton of new paths that I never foresaw. I find these new possibil-ities unimaginably fascinating."

I was appalled that Marcus looked like he'd just won the lottery.

"But enough chit chat, Dani. It's time for us to go for a little boat ride. Ta-ta, sweetheart." He slammed the door of his cabin closed and locked me inside before I could react. I pounded on the door, but I only heard him laughing at me.

I slid my phone out of my pocket to see a missed text message from Luke letting me know that he was waiting at Alice's house. Could he get to the marina in time if I sent a new message? I moved away from the door, hoping Marcus wouldn't see through the window what I was doing. But just as I was about to hit reply and send my SOS to Luke, the door opened. Marcus took the few steps to reach me and grabbed my phone.

"No need for this." He tossed it through the door. It bounced on the deck once and went over the rail, splashing into the ocean.

What would I do now?

With the door ajar and Marcus still facing me, Pip wiggled through. Like a white torpedo, she launched herself at the unsuspecting murderer.

"What the—" Marcus yelled, swatting at Pip who nimbly jumped away from his swipes. Her quick unpredictable moves kept Marcus spinning in circles.

"Get him, Pip," I encouraged. "Good girl."

While Pip had Marcus completely disoriented, I lunged for an air horn hanging next to the cabin door. Immediately, I went out the door and

squeezed the button for dear life, praying someone
at the marina would come to my aid. Over and over
I pushed the button while keeping an eye on Pip
and Marcus inside the cabin.

With one elegant bound, Pip hurtled through the
door, joining me on the deck. I slammed the door
closed and turned the key that was still inserted in
the lock. Marcus oriented himself enough and heave
himself against door.

But the door held.

I could breathe again, but as my legs turned to
jelly, I leaned on the boat railing, blasting the air
horn again and again, afraid to end the racket until
someone arrived.

Pip leaped off the boat and ran down the dock
toward Kyle's office building. If he didn't pay attention to the air horn, he was about to get an earful
from one fired up terrier.

Once I could stand without collapsing, I double-
checked that the door still held against Marcus's
constant pounding. Then I went to Brent's boat to
let Misty out. She wagged her tail and danced
around me like she'd never been happier to see a
human. I was honored.

Kyle, leading Luke and AJ down the dock,
rushed toward Misty and me. Pip nipped at AJ's

heels to keep them all moving quickly. Not that they needed her extra incentive.

"What's going on, Dani?" AJ yelled. "What's all the racket about?"

"It's Marcus," I managed to say, thinking that was enough.

They all looked at me with question mark expressions.

"*Marcus* is the killer. He was planning to kill me too and dump me in the ocean." Just saying the words out loud made me shudder at how close I'd come to becoming fish food.

"Marcus?" Luke asked once he had me wrapped in his arms. "How did you figure it out?"

"He knew how Wilhelmina was murdered. He knew she was speared with her sign. There's a whole blog post in his cabin framing me for the murder." I slumped against Luke, never wanting to leave his embrace.

"It's okay," he whispered as he rubbed my back. "It's over now."

He held me, while Pip sat on one side and Misty sat on the other, and we all waited while AJ read Marcus his rights, handcuffed him, and marched him off the dock to the police car.

The built-up tension and fear drained away with every step that Marcus took away from me.

"I'll take Misty to Alice's house, if you don't mind," Kyle said. "It's the least I can do after what you've been through.

"And I'll take you home," Luke said. "AJ told me he could catch up with your statement another time."

"I love the sound of that."

37

*S*unday morning rewarded me with one of those perfect October New England days —cool and sunny with the fall reds, oranges, and yellows glowing brilliantly.

While I sat on the patio at Sea Breeze with a blanket around my shoulders and Pip resting under my chair, Blueberry Bay shimmered in front of me. Boats bobbed, waves gently crashed, and seagulls soared to add a helping of soothing magic for my frazzled nerves.

Finally, everything on the surface *and* below was back to normal.

I let out a deep sigh of satisfaction.

"Tea?"

"And I thought I was already enjoying the

perfect morning. Having tea served to me tops it off," I said to Rose. Somehow, I knew she'd hover over me for a while.

She poured tea for both of us and treated Pip to a dog bone. As she settled in the chair next to me, she said, "Chad and Christy are all set at the diner. That gives us plenty of time to discuss the final plans for my apartment."

"Not—"

She raised her finger and shushed me with a stare over the top of her glasses. "No interruptions, Danielle. Luke will be here soon, and together, we'll put the final touches on my grandmother-in-law apartment. I'm ready for a small cozy space that Trouble and I can have to ourselves."

"You don't want to share with us after we get married?" I didn't want her to feel shuffled out of her beautiful home.

"Sea Breeze belongs to you, Danielle. I won't listen to any more excuses. What I do want is for you to get over your silly idea that you're pushing me aside."

"I—"

Her raised finger silenced me again. "Trouble and I will be perfectly comfortable. You haven't even looked at Luke's plans yet. I think you'll be surprised. I'll have an amazing view with a sunny living room, which is what I care about most, a compact kitchen, a cozy bedroom, and he insisted on a large bathroom with a walk-in bathtub thing-a-ma-jiggy." Rose nudged me with her elbow. "He must think I'm getting old."

"I never said that." Luke's steps tapped on the patio behind us.

"And you promised not to sneak up on us while we're in the middle of our girl talk," Rose said with a lightness in her voice that reminded me how much she loved Luke.

Another set of footsteps tapped across the stones. Was I surprised at all the visitors? Not at all.

"I brought your favorite, Dani." Lily placed a box on my lap. "Actually, I'm thinking it might be your *newest* favorite since you haven't actually had this creation yet."

I opened the lid. An almond and raspberry aroma drifted to my nose making me drool with anticipation. I helped myself to the largest square and passed the box to Rose.

"I had an order for an almond dessert, and this is what I came up with—Raspberry Almond bars. What do you think?"

I nodded enthusiastically since my mouth was

full of Lily's latest winner, leaving me unable to tell her it tasted like a piece of heaven.

"Are we late?" Sue Ellen asked. Of course, she and Maggie weren't going to be left out of any gathering, impromptu or not.

Sue Ellen leaned over and kissed my cheek. "Bless your heart, Dani. You had us all *sick* with worry."

"AJ can't come, but he asked if you'd stop at the station later to give him your statement," Maggie said. "What's in the box?" Without waiting for an answer, she grabbed a square for herself. "Any coffee around this place?"

"Just tea," Rose said.

I hid a chuckle behind my hand, knowing Maggie and tea weren't much of a duo.

"I'll make coffee," Lily offered. "I'm sure someone else will want some, too."

Rose harrumphed. "So much for our quiet cup of tea together, Danielle. This is *exactly* why I need my own corner apartment."

"Okay. Okay. I give up. Whatever you want is fine with me." After all, I told myself, Rose wasn't moving across town. Her brand spanking new apartment would still be part of Sea Breeze, just with its own separate entryway.

I settled back on my chair with one hand dangling down, resting on Pip. The other held my delicious mint tea.

The conversation drifted around me like an old wool sweater — snug, comforting, and warm. I was content to listen as Luke shared more details about my Lobster Trash Trap plan. I was thrilled to hear everyone embracing it with loud approvals.

"With all the excitement," Rose said. "I almost forgot about this important decision about the Best Business Award."

I tensed with anticipation, expecting to hear that I'd won.

The committee unanimously decided to present the award to the Savory Soup & Sandwich Café. They said he needs the most help to get back on his feet."

I opened one eye and then I grinned. "Perfect!"

"And," Rose continued, "the Blueberry Bay Grapevine has pledged to match the one thousand dollar prize money that goes with the award, and I plan to challenge other businesses in town to do the same. Together, we can help each other and keep Misty Harbor a destination for tourists. The challenge will go out in the next issue of the Grapevine."

I nodded in agreement. Rose always saw the big picture.

"Dani?" Maggie said. "Are we still on for tonight?"

I leaned forward in my chair. "Tonight? Oh, yes. Of course. I'm picking you up at six, right?"

"Yup. And I hope you have something special planned because I only turn thirty once."

"Oh, it will be special. Don't worry." I still wasn't convinced it would be her idea of special, but that was AJ's problem.

For the rest of the day, I meandered through a walk on the beach with Luke and Pip, a visit to the diner for lunch, and gave my statement to AJ.

"Marcus really had an elaborate plan," AJ said when I'd finished with my details. "He also admitted that he set the fire in his own boat with some smoldering paper and plastic to make all the smoke. It gave him time to leave and make it look like he'd only returned to the marina when he saw Kyle. I do think he was planning to make you disappear, Dani. And all for something to write on his blog."

"And protect himself, his marijuana habit, and the customers he supplied. Did he tell you about that?" I asked.

AJ's eyebrows rose in surprise. He jotted something on the paper in front of him. "He didn't, but that's a nice touch to add to all of his charges."

"Poor Wilhelmina," I said. "As big of a pain in the neck that she was, she meant well."

AJ closed the file in front of him and folded his hands together. "Are the plans all set for Maggie's party tonight?"

"All set and now you'll be able to stay?"

"Yes, thanks to you."

"And Pip."

Pip wagged her tail and jumped on my lap.

"See you tonight."

"I wouldn't miss it for anything." AJ, in an uncharacteristic gesture, hugged me when I stood up. "You take care of yourself, Danielle Rose. This town wouldn't be the same without you."

I walked out, not wanting him to see the tears in my eyes.

*J*ust like I promised, I picked Maggie up at her apartment at six. She had on a slinky dress, short wool jacket, and ankle boots which contrasted with my jeans, sweater, and a scarf to jazz it up a bit. I planned for comfort, not fashion.

"So, what's the plan?" she asked. I could hear excitement in her voice. I guess she intended to make the most of her special day with or without AJ.

"First, I thought we'd stop at Sea Breeze for drinks with Rose, Lily, and Sue Ellen. Then, I've got reservations for dinner. But that destination is a surprise."

"You know I hate surprises, Dani."

"Sorry. Take it or leave it."

"Okay. But it had better be worth it."

We drove the twisty road to Sea Breeze, chatting about this and that but mostly Maggie talked about AJ and the kittens. I couldn't believe how domestic she was becoming, but maybe it had something to do with turning thirty.

"Ready for that drink?" I asked.

"You betcha, girly." She laughed so hard I was afraid she might wet her pants. I was pretty sure she'd already had a birthday celebration drink on her own.

"Are you alright, Maggie?"

"Never been better." She winked at me.

"Okay, then." I sure hoped I wasn't leading her into something she'd hate me for later.

I opened the door and crossed my fingers while Maggie walked into the silence.

We made the short walk to the living room. I held my breath waiting for the big *SURPRISE*.

It was a surprise all right.

But not the one *I'd* been expecting.

All my friends stood in a semi-circle around a table loaded with presents. BRIDAL SHOWER in big, bright letters taped to the front of the table fluttered as Pip darted from under the table straight to me. Her purple bandana covered with white daisies, was a nice touch.

"Huh?" I stared while my brain worked at catching up with reality.

And then chaos broke out. Everyone yelled "*SURPRISE*," and surrounded me with hugs and kisses. Maggie pushed me forward to a chair covered in a white shimmery fabric. Someone placed a crown on my head.

"It's not your birthday, Maggie?" My brain struggled as I tried to figure this all out.

"Yeah, it is, but AJ and I will do something another time. I *hate* surprises."

Everyone laughed.

Luke handed me a glass of blueberry cordial and whispered. "The surprise is on you."

Yeah, I had to admit, they'd pulled off the surprise of a lifetime, and I intended to enjoy every second of it.

I hope you enjoyed this book.

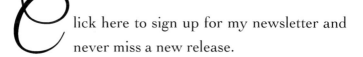lick here to sign up for my newsletter and never miss a new release.

MORE BLUEBERRY BAY

Welcome to Blueberry Bay, a scenic region of Maine peppered with quaint small towns and home to a shocking number of mysteries. If you loved this book, then make sure to check out its sister series from other talented Cozy Mystery authors...

Pet Whisperer P.I.
By Molly Fitz

Glendale is home to Blueberry Bay's first ever talking cat detective. Along with his ragtag gang of human and animal helpers, Octo-Cat is determined to save the day... so long as it doesn't interfere with his schedule. Start with book one, *Kitty Confidential*,

which is now available to buy or borrow!
Visit www.MollyMysteries.com for more.

Little Dog Diner
By Emmie Lyn

Misty Harbor boasts the best lobster rolls in all of
Blueberry Bay. There's another thing that's always
on the menu, too. Murder! Dani and her little
terrier, Pip, have a knack for being in the wrong
place at the wrong time… which often lands them
smack in the middle of a fresh, new murder mystery
and in the crosshairs of one cunning criminal after
the next. Start with book one, *Mixing Up Murder*,
which is now available to buy or borrow!
Visit www.EmmieLynBooks.com for more.

Shelf Indulgence
By S.E. Babin

Dewdrop Springs is home to Tattered Pages, a
popular bookshop with an internet cafe, a grumpy
Persian cat named Poppy, and some of the most
suspicious characters you'll ever meet. And poor
Dakota Adair has just inherited it all. She'll need to

make peace with her new cat and use all her book smarts to catch a killer or she might be the next to wind up dead in the stacks. Book one, *Hardback Homicide,* will be coming soon. Keep an eye on www.QuirkyCozy.com for more.

Haunted Housekeeping
By R.A. Muth

Cooper's Cove is home to Blueberry Bay's premier estate cleaning service. Tori and Hazel, the ill-fated proprietors of Bubbles and Troubles, are prepared to uncover a few skeletons. But when a real one turns up, they'll have to solve the mystery quickly if they're going to save their reputations--and their lives. Book one, *The Squeaky Clean Skeleton,* will be coming soon. Keep an eye on www.QuirkyCozy.com for more.

The Kindergarten Coven
By F.M. Storm

Quiet, secluded, and most importantly, far away from his annoying magical family, Guy couldn't wait to start a new life on Caraway Island.

Unfortunately, he hadn't counted on his four-year-old daughter coming into her own witchy powers early… or on her accidentally murdering one of the PTO moms. Oops! Book one, *Stay-at-Home Sorcery,* will be coming soon. Keep an eye on www.QuirkyCozy.com for more.

MORE EMMIE!

I hope you enjoyed this book.

Click here to sign up for my newsletter and never miss a new release.

∅Ψ∅

About Emmie Lyn

Emmie Lyn shares her world with her husband, a rescue terrier named Underdog, and a black cat named Ziggy. When she's not busy thinking of ways to kill off a character, she loves enjoying tea and chocolate in her flower garden, hiking, or spending time near the ocean. Find out more at Emmielynbooks.com.

∅Ψ∅

More from Emmie

COZY MYSTERIES

Little Dog Diner

Mixing Up Murder

Serving Up Suspects

Dishing Up Deceit

Cooking Up Chaos

🍴

COMING SOON

Crumbling Up Crooks

Dicing Up Disaster

🍴

ROMANTIC SUSPENSE

Gold Coast Retrievers

Helping Hanna

Shielding Shelly

Made in the USA
Monee, IL
31 October 2019